Bonjour Shanghai

BONJOUR GIRL

Bonjour Shanghai

ISABELLE LAFLÈCHE

DUNDURN
TORONTO

Publisher: Scott Fraser | Editor: Jess Shulman
Cover designer: Laura Boyle
Cover image: ©istock.com/alvaher
Printer: Webcom, a division of Marquis Book Printing Inc.

Library and Archives Canada Cataloguing in Publication

Title: Bonjour Shanghai / Isabelle Laflèche.
Names: Laflèche, Isabelle, 1970- author.
Description: Series statement: Bonjour girl
Identifiers: Canadiana (print) 20190072598 | Canadiana (ebook) 20190072601 | ISBN 9781459742314 (softcover) | ISBN 9781459742321 (PDF) | ISBN 9781459742338 (epub)
Classification: LCC PS8623.A35825 B66 2019 | DDC jC813/.6—dc23

We acknowledge the support of the Canada Council for the Arts and the Ontario Arts Council for our publishing program. We also acknowledge the financial support of the Government of Ontario, through the Ontario Book Publishing Tax Credit and Ontario Creates, and the Government of Canada.

Care has been taken to trace the ownership of copyright material used in this book. The author and the publisher welcome any information enabling them to rectify any references or credits in subsequent editions.

The publisher is not responsible for websites or their content unless they are owned by the publisher.

Printed and bound in Canada.

VISIT US AT

 dundurn.com | @dundurnpress |  dundurnpress | dundurnpress

Dundurn
3 Church Street, Suite 500
Toronto, Ontario, Canada
M5E 1M2

For Dominique

To my child's eyes, which had seen nothing else, Shanghai was a waking dream where everything I could imagine had already been taken to its extreme.
— J.G. Ballard, *The Kindness of Women*

Prologue

I MADE IT.

Well, barely.

I ran down the airline ramp all sweaty and winded, my bags swinging from side to side, including the canvas bag Jake gave me as a goodbye present that reads *Smart Women Don't Kiss Ass, They Kick It* in bold pink.

I almost missed my flight because deep down inside, I still wasn't sure I should leave. It was no surprise that leaving Jonathan behind was heart-wrenching. We stood there holding each other in the middle of the busy JFK terminal for what felt like forever, with Jake looking on.

Even though I was trying to be fully present in Jonathan's arms, I could see and feel Jake's anxiety in the distance. He kept checking his phone. I wish I could have helped resolve all his problems before I left, but I just couldn't.

We all came together for a group hug, and I promised to video-call them daily on WeChat, then I kissed them both and just ran and didn't look back until I got to the security gate. That's probably why I'd chosen to wear sneak-ers — so I could run. Maybe I'd known that if I slowed down, I might lose my resolve in an instant, change my plans, and never get on that plane. Love and friendship can open your heart wide and make you do foolish things.

But I just couldn't do that to Maddie, to my parents, or, more importantly, to myself. I need to prove that I can kick ass on my own. That I really can make it.

I rushed through security and dashed off to the gate with my visa, passport, and boarding pass in hand, and now here I am at the plane. I don't look anything like a Parsons or Condé Nast fashion student at the moment, with sweat dripping from my forehead and my hair in a messy bun, but who cares?

When I board, the flight attendants don't look too thrilled about my tardiness. But their mood shifts when I compliment them on their uniforms: impeccable red dresses and delicate silk scarves tied around their necks. They look impossibly chic.

Some of the passengers shoot me evil stares, maybe because I'm late, but more likely because of the pink-sloganed bag I keep shoving in their faces as I awk-wardly manoeuvre to my seat. Jake would be immensely proud.

I pull out my magazines, the two paperbacks Jonathan gave me to read, and my bottled water. I also have a box of cupcakes baked for me by Jake's mom. I actually teared up when he handed them to me. The fact that Jake's mom has no clue about her son's predicament breaks my heart.

I look around. Thankfully, my seat neighbour is a mature-looking Chinese woman who's already got her nose in a book. I like my travel companions to be quiet so I can read and write.

I'm hoping to finally write another blog post for *Bonjour Girl*, one that resonates with my values, now that I have the time, space, and energy to do it.

After the emergency protocols have been duly explained and we've taken off, I pull out my laptop. I open a bag of roasted almonds and think about what to write. This feels good. Taking refuge in my writing will help me to have a more positive outlook on my upcoming adventure. I'm going to Shanghai!

Someone taps me on the shoulder.

"Clementine? Clementine Liu?"

I look up to see a handsome young Asian man standing next to me in the aisle.

"I have a note for you from a close friend of mine," he says, handing me a folded piece of paper. "Enjoy your flight, okay?"

"Thanks."

I sit up straight, curious about this mysterious note.

I open it and my eyes nearly pop out of their sockets when I see who it's from.

Welcome to Shanghai.

Chapter One

I WAKE UP to the faint ping of my phone. I forgot to put it in silent mode after a late night of school work. I get up to go fetch it from a console in the next room; I've started to follow a no-phone-at-night policy.

There's a red circle on the top right-hand corner of my Instagram icon notifying me of a new message. I bring my phone back to my bedroom — really, I should say, to the spare room of my cousin Maddie's apartment — and sit up in my bed, propping myself up with fluffy pillows. Last semester, I moved from Paris, where my mother is an opera singer and my father owns a clothing and rare books shop, to New York City to attend the Parsons School of Design. Maddie, my mother's cousin and a teacher at Parsons, offered me the spare room of her cool Williamsburg loft and promised my father she'd look out for me. At the moment, she's out of town travelling for work, so I have the place to myself.

Given the early hour, I assume the message is from my best friend, Jake, sharing a cool fashion design or a hilarious post, or Maddie sharing an inspirational quote. She just can't help doing that kind of thing. Or maybe it's my boyfriend, Jonathan, sharing some of his beautiful photography.

I open the message and find that I'm totally off base. It's an unfamiliar account belonging to an Asian man with great hair, and an amazing smile.

> Hey Clementine! I'm Henry Lee, a student at the Conde Nast Center in Shanghai. I heard you'll be joining us, so I just wanted to reach out and say hello. Nice feed, BTW. You have a quirky style I really like! Are you planning to be a fashion designer? I look forward to learning more about you. See you soon!

I roll my eyes and sigh. Not everyone who attends fashion school wants to be a designer. That's so clichéd. I don't have the talent or the desire. Hasn't this guy read my profile, which says that I dream of becoming a fashion journalist? Still, the fact that he likes my style makes me smile. I guess news that I'm going to be part of the Shanghai exchange program has gotten around. I decide to scroll through Henry's account. That's what fashion students do — we check out each other's style online. Not because we're shallow, but because we're a community and find each other inspirational.

My heart stops for a second when I see his account. It's filled with pictures of stunning locally made clothes, quotes about protecting the environment, and travel photos. Judging by his impressive feed, he must travel extensively. I've read that accessing Instagram from inside China can be tricky. Over the past decade, the Chinese government has blocked Google, Facebook, Twitter, Instagram, the *New York Times*, and thousands of other foreign websites. A bunch of Chinese websites serve the same function instead. Henry must post on Instagram while he's out of the country. I've also heard that it's possible to visit external websites from within China by using a virtual private network, or VPN.

There's one particularly beautiful photo of Henry standing in the desert of Jaisalmer in India. He's wearing a hat and a white shirt, a pair of torn jeans, and a bold fuchsia pashmina silk scarf. Again, I'm taken by his smile, and the scenery takes my breath away.

I can't help myself. Within seconds, I find myself pulled in.

So I scroll.

And I scroll some more.

His sense of visual storytelling, something we learned about during our first semester at Parsons, is impeccable, a powerful mix of fashion, eco-consciousness, and nature shots. That's basically what all Instagram users are doing — storytelling. We're creating a persona, of sorts, and telling the world about our little corner of the universe and our vision of ourselves. Henry's writing is insightful, too. I like what I see.

This thought makes my heart flutter a beat, and within a nanosecond, I think of Jonathan. What am I doing?

I'm hit with a pang of guilt. I need to stop scrolling right now. I'm dating an amazing guy who's totally loving and kind. I shouldn't be interested in anyone else.

A ton of questions barrel through my mind. Is what I'm doing considered cheating? Is it more than just curiosity? What is it called, anyway? Is there a term for it?

I tell myself there's nothing wrong with what I'm doing, really. Henry reached out to me, and my looking through his profile is just research about the exchange program in China. Right?

Probably not. Henry is looking forward to meeting me in Shanghai. So no, it's not the same thing. I need to stop this now.

I turn off my phone. It's way too much guilt and too many questions for my foggy brain this early in the morning. I'll answer Henry's message later, after school, maybe, once I've had a chance to think about it.

We'll see what the future brings.

For now, I'll just focus on finishing my second semester in New York and then getting myself to Shanghai for the summer term without any major hiccups or drama.

And that's enough work for one day, isn't it?

Hey Henry, thanks for your message.
Looking forward to Shanghai! I may
need some tips about the city when I
get there. I'm half-French, half-Chinese,
but I've never been to Shanghai. BTW,
I noticed your interest in eco-fashion.
That's awesome, it's one of the topics I
like to write about on my blog, Bonjour
Girl. See you soon! Take care,

Clementine

I notice that he's online. Within seconds, I receive a response. I feel my pulse quickening.

> Oh hello! Great to hear from you, Clementine. I'll be happy to provide all the tips you need. I was born in Hong Kong, studied in New York, and have been living in Shanghai for a few years. It's a really cool place! And I actually read your blog already. I'm a fan of your writing and all those great interviews. Keep it up!
>
> H.

He's a fan of my writing. He reads my blog. He likes my quirky style. He's devastatingly handsome. He's interested in protecting the environment.

The best thing to do is forget this exchange ever happened. Or at least try to forget this exchange ever happened. No, I'm definitely going to forget this exchange ever happened.

Well, I'm going to do my very best to forget it ever happened.

Chapter Two

"HEY, CLEM. What's up with the goofy smile?" Jake asks as he sits down next to me in class. He's wearing a white hoodie, black track pants, and his funky sneakers with the silver stars.

"Huh?" I jump a little in my seat, obviously distracted. "Oh, it's nothing."

"Don't tell me it's nothing, sistah. I know you better than the inside of a Ruffles chip bag." He twirls his pencil and grins. "Are you dreaming about pretty boy again?"

"Um, I guess. Jonathan and I are having dinner tonight."

"Oh, cool. Whereabouts?"

"Some new sushi place near his apartment."

"Ooooh. How very convenient." He raises his eyebrows suggestively.

I'm crazy about Jonathan, but for some reason, this morning, I can't get Instagram Henry out of my mind. He's good-looking, there's no doubt about it, but it's more than that. It probably has something to do with my blog. It's like we both share the same goal: to use our social media platforms to raise awareness of sustainability issues in the fashion industry, and to educate the public about eco-fashion and how to be responsible consumers. It's refreshing to meet someone with a similar ideology to mine.

But I have to try to forget about Henry. I need to focus on my relationship, my fashion marketing class, and getting through this semester. We're two thirds of the way through already, and I need to maintain my focus all the way to the finish line. A fascinating course in an exciting new place awaits, and lots of people are counting on me to do well.

Our teacher enters the classroom. His name is Brian Reynolds, and he's a former Seventh Avenue marketing executive. He teaches us about the ins and outs of branding, which is critical in our industry.

Jake loves this class. He applies the concepts we learn to his own personal design project. He's creating a clothing line for people in wheelchairs, and so far, he's received lots of praise from classmates, faculty members, and Instagram users.

"So how's the collection going?" I ask him.

"It's coming along nicely. I've added a few more pieces. Can't you tell from the dark circles under my eyes?"

He does look tired, but I won't mention it. I know how sensitive he is about his usually fresh complexion.

"You're not getting enough sleep."

"I know, babycakes. But between work, school, and pursuing my dreams, it's been intense."

He looks away, avoiding my gaze. I have a feeling he's not telling me the entire story.

"Anything else bothering you?"

"Yeah, you could say that. Finances are tight. I could use some more moolah. Expenses are through the roof, and I spent the last of my scholarship money on fabrics last semester."

My heart sinks. I wish I could do something to help him out, but I'm not exactly rolling in it, either. I'm barely making ends meet with my allowance, and I'm trying to save some money for my trip to Shanghai.

"But don't worry about me, pussycat. I have ways of making ends meet and getting shit done. I'm a master manifestor," he says, still twirling his glitter pencil.

"Of course you are. You always get what you need. You're my hero."

He looks away. For some reason, my compliment is making him uncomfortable.

I get it, though. Money problems can suck the life out of you. I saw my father go through it a few years ago, when his store in Paris ran into financial problems after the terrorist attacks. Tourism nosedived and sales slumped to zero. It was a tough time for all of us, and we were scared, but also defiant — we weren't about to let the actions of some ill-intentioned fanatics define our lives.

"How about meeting for a giant pretzel after class?" I ask Jake.

"Sorry, hon, not today. I got stuff to take care of," he says, lost in his thoughts. I can tell he's stressed. Jake rarely turns down a snack.

"Hey, guys, can I have a word before class starts?"

We look up to see Brian standing in front of us.

I'm intrigued. "Sure."

"Of course you can, sir," Jake says admiringly. Brian is so ruggedly handsome, he could be a model in a Nautica billboard ad. He's wearing a tan sports jacket, a striped crewneck T-shirt, and a bandana around his neck. The only thing missing is a sailboat.

Brian nods toward the door and we follow him out to the hallway.

"Listen, I just wanted to share some observations." We hunch forward like football players leaning in to discuss strategy as students stream by us.

"I'm only saying this because I care about you guys and I want to see you kick ass out in the real world, okay?" Jake and I nod in sync. We're getting a pep talk. It's all good.

"I was there at the awards ceremony when you won your award last semester, Jake, and when you received an honourable mention, Clementine. That was great work and well earned. But now, expectations are high, and as trailblazers, you need to lead the way. To keep impressing the Parsons faculty, you've got to push yourselves outside of your comfort zone. Try different things." He looks at us expectantly. Again, Jake and I both nod. As he describes the pressure we're under, I can almost feel it mounting.

"For example, Jake, you could broaden your project by creating samples not only for people in wheelchairs, but also for people with different types of disabilities."

Jake's face falls. I know this suggestion is unexpected, and he certainly doesn't need the extra work. But after a moment, he nods at Brian.

"And Clementine, you could try something new on *Bonjour Girl*. Maybe interview designers after their shows, around town, at home, from their showrooms ... even film live interviews. Then you can link to their sites and those of their business partners and get a cut from any online sales they generate through your links. It's called affiliated selling — there's money in it, and the possibilities are endless."

I find myself nodding like Jake did, even though something in the back of my mind says no. This sounds too commercial, not what I had in mind when I launched my blog. I prefer to discuss social issues as they relate to the fashion industry, without a direct profit objective. How can I remain objective if I follow Brian's suggestion? Affiliated marketing sounds like crass commercialization.

"Both of you are on the cutting edge of what I teach in this class. Thinking outside the box like this is what'll take you places, I promise. And I want both of you to succeed, not only on paper, but in the real world, too. I want you to be financially successful. Does that make sense?" Brian asks.

I nod. I want to show my willingness to explore new ideas, but what he's suggesting is hardly thinking outside the box. He wants to see more varied content on my site, and I guess he has a point. But all this talk of making money from sales makes me uneasy. On the bright side, it's rewarding to be singled out by a Parsons teacher who's interested in my blog and wants me to succeed. I'm just uncertain about changing the editorial direction of *Bonjour Girl*. I've put so much effort into creating a unique, independent voice to distinguish my content from that of other bloggers. I'm not sure I want to change it.

But what Brian is saying isn't criticism — it's encouragement, and there's a difference.

Jake and I look at each other. There's both excitement and panic in my friend's eyes. I'm sure the thought of being financially successful is appealing, but he's probably not keen about dealing with even greater pressure and workload. The lack of sleep must be getting to him. I know how driven Jake is, and I worry that Brian's comments will cause him to push himself even further when he can barely handle things now.

"Thanks for your support, and for the advice," I finally say. "I really value your opinion, Brian."

"Yeah, thanks," Jake chimes in.

"My pleasure. I call it like I see it. And I see success in your futures, so keep it up, okay?" He smiles and heads back into class.

I just wish there were more than twenty-four hours in a day. But, like Jake, I'll find a way. I always do.

"Jake, I'm having second thoughts," I say after we're back in our seats.

"What about?"

"Going to Shanghai."

"Whaddya mean? Being selected for the Condé Nast summer classes is like winning the frickin' lottery! You're going to one of the best fashion programs in the world. Are you off your rocker?"

"No, I'm just stressed out about it. It's so unfair that only I get to go when there are other talented people just as deserving. What if people think I got preferential treatment because I'm related to a Parsons teacher? What if I get bullied again? I don't think I could take it."

"Oh, stop it. Just because some asshole bullied you here in New York doesn't mean it'll happen in Shanghai. I'm sure the people are far more civilized there — not like in this crazy place."

"Right ... maybe that's not the only reason I'm having doubts," I finally admit.

"What is it, then? Oh wait, I bet it has to do with lover boy."

He can see right through me. "Uh, well, maybe." I hate to admit it, but I *am* worried about my relationship with Jonathan. Long-distance dating can be tough. The stats say that the chances of surviving it are slim.

"What are you worried about, pumpkin?" Jake asks patiently.

But I remain silent. I can't put my feelings into words. I have mixed feelings about my boyfriend's job, which involves taking pictures of beautiful fashion models. Leaving him behind in New York is going to be tough on my spirit. And then there's the time difference. Will we survive this?

"Babe," Jake says finally, "you have adventures waiting for you in Asia. Stop wasting your precious energy worrying about some dude, okay? Besides, haven't you heard the old saying?"

"Which one?"

"If a woman hasn't met the right man by the time she's twenty-four, she may be *very* lucky."

"Nice try." His joke falls flat. I know Jake thinks I should focus on my future, not my boyfriend, but I just can't help it.

"What's the problem, Clemy?" he asks softly, this time without any sarcasm.

"I don't know, I'm worried he'll lose interest or something."

"Oh, geez. Do I need to remind you that he's already professed his love for you *and* given you a piece of family jewellery? I mean, you need to quit that shit, girl. It doesn't look good on you."

I go silent again. I know he's right. I hate feeling this way — it sucks.

"Listen, I have tickets to a Broadway show this week, a gift from my godmother. Let Uncle Jake take you out for a night on the town. Whaddya say?"

"That sounds amazing! Forget what I said. I'm over it already," I say, resolving to focus on all that's positive.

The question is, can I?

Chapter Three

ACCORDING TO FAMOUS Hollywood costume designer Edith Head, "You can have anything you want in life if you dress for it."

I'm following her advice as I pick out an outfit for my date with Jonathan. I haven't seen him much since he got back from Italy, and I'm really excited to meet him for a quiet dinner in Williamsburg, just the two of us. I want to dazzle him in a low-key sensual way, especially since our days together before I head off to Asia are numbered.

Instead of wearing one of my usual second-hand finds, I slip into a pair of slim black jeans, a flowy, light-pink tunic, and a necklace made of mala beads. It's a softer look than what I usually wear. I add some light-pink velvet platform shoes. I'm happy with the result: it's feminine and sexy. I know it's a look he likes, as he often features styles like this in his photo shoots. I spray some light perfume on my wrists and behind my ears, then take a picture of my outfit in the full-length mirror and text it to Jake. Within seconds, I receive a heart, a smiley face, and a thumbs-up. He also sends me a close-up of himself winking. This cracks me up.

What I'm keeping hidden from my best friend and (for now) from my boyfriend is my brand-new lingerie.

On Instagram, I recently came across a beautiful line of hand-embroidered lingerie, and decided to splurge. The bra features two embroidered hands holding daisies, and the panties have an embroidered sparrow on them. The look is feminine, dreamy, and sweetly seductive. It's also the type of handmade, sustainable fashion I like to talk about on my blog and in my social media. I like to test the merchandise before I sing its praises.

Growing up, I always admired my mother's vast collection of lingerie. I never gave it too much thought for myself, though, despite my mom trying her hardest to get me to wear lacy things instead of simple cotton briefs and tank tops.

In Paris, she'd take me to the Galeries Lafayette, but I always preferred the shoe section. I guess spending a lot of money on something hidden baffled me — but now that Jonathan is in my life, I see things differently. I like the feeling of having something sexy under my clothes, something that tantalizes the senses; it makes me feel more confident and love my body more. I guess I have my mother to thank. She totally owns her goddess-like charms. That probably explains why men flock to her in droves. Including my ex-boyfriend. But I'm over that.

Tantalizing Jonathan tonight has been on my mind, and I'm sure it's been on his mind, too.

I want to be prepared. A woman should always be prepared.

After putting on some lip gloss and a touch of mascara, I take one last peek in the mirror, brush my hair, and fly out the door.

We'll see if this embroidered lace works its magic.

"You look gorgeous, Clem," Jonathan says as soon as I arrive at the restaurant. He's waiting for me at the bar. He holds my face in his hands, kisses me, and stares at me with a look that's more intense than I'm used to. Can he feel the sensuality emanating from my hidden underthings?

"Thanks, so do you," I say, taking off my jean jacket and taking a seat.

"What would you like to drink? The usual? A glass of red?"

"That sounds great. How was your day?"

"Good. Lots of new work coming in that'll bring me some cash to pay for my flight to Shanghai. I'm already planning my visit."

"Fantastic! That's music to my ears," I say, thrilled by the prospect of seeing Jonathan in China. It makes me feel less conflicted about leaving New York.

He orders, putting a hand on my leg. He leans in and kisses me on the lips again, this time lingering longer. This sends shockwaves through my body. I guess he can feel something's different with me. My new lingerie is making me feel more feminine and kicking my desire into overdrive. I should have listened to my mother and done this ages ago. Despite my reluctance to admit it, she's usually right about these things.

"Do you want to eat here at the bar? It might be fun."

"Sure."

"We can get oysters." He winks.

"Yes!" I say, excited. I love oysters. My dad introduced them to me when we used to take day trips to Normandy.

Jonathan puts his hand on the nape of my neck and rubs his thumb up and down, sending a frisson down my spine. I wonder how long I'll last before I melt completely, like the ice in the mojito in front of him.

Before I can visualize a passionate, sultry encounter, his phone buzzes. He picks it up and looks at it, then abruptly stands up, looking perplexed, even panicked.

"Oh, man, I'm so sorry, Clem. This is urgent. I gotta take this."

He paces the entire length of the bar as he talks, nervously running his fingers through his hair. What could be so pressing? What could be putting such a frown on that sweet face?

After a few minutes, he finally walks over, looking distraught. My stomach drops. Whatever is happening, it's not good.

"I'm really sorry, Clem, but I need to go. It's an emergency."

"What's going on? Is everything okay?" A million images flash through my mind as I try to grasp this change in events. I hope nothing bad has happened to any of his family.

"I'll explain later. Don't worry, okay? I'll make it up to you, love, I promise." He kisses me on the side of the head, looking as though he's already checked out. "Do you want to invite Jake over for dinner instead? I'm happy to pay for it."

Jake? As much as I love my best friend, he's not exactly what I had in mind for tonight. What a buzzkill. I shake my head.

"Nah, it's okay, I'll just finish my wine and head home. I'm only a few blocks away. I'm behind on some school work, anyway. Don't worry, I'll be fine."

"I'll call you later, okay? I'm really, really sorry." He kisses me on the head again and dashes toward the exit.

"Sure, no problem," I mutter. What on earth could be so pressing?

Once I get home, I decide to take a bath to forget about the sad turn of events.

I turn on the faucet and pour some coconut bath oil into the water. As I wait for the tub to fill up, I let my hair down and play "Express Yourself," one of my favourite Madonna hits from the 80s, on Spotify. I sway from side to side, pick up a hairbrush, and sing into it, playfully dancing in my new underwear. A night in alone might be second best, but I'm going to make the most of it with self-care and lighthearted fun. This will have to do for tonight. If nothing else, it'll help alleviate some of the doubts swirling around in my head.

Chapter Four

"HEY, CLEMY, WHAT'S UP?" Jake says, sitting down next to me. We've got a fashion history class, but before the teacher can tell us about the past, we need to discuss my future.

Jake is wearing a sweatshirt with the words *Eat More Kale* printed in dark green, which is hilarious because Jake never eats kale. He doesn't care much for greens. He's more into pink cupcakes, mustard pretzels, and brownies. I wish he *would* eat kale — it would be much better for his health.

"So Jonathan was weird last night. I'm not sure what to make of it," I whisper. I don't want my other classmates to know about my personal life. They already know plenty about me as it is, thanks to a bullying situation that escalated into a real *merde* show last semester. I'm trying to stay under the radar now, even though my bestie is larger than life and can often be very loud.

"Oh, tell me more." He slinks forward, sliding his arms over his desk to get closer.

"He got a phone call, said something was urgent, and disappeared. He just left me at the bar. We haven't talked since. He texted me this morning but was super vague. He barely mentioned last night. This isn't like him."

"Stuff happens, Clem. It's New York, people get busy. He'll make it up to you, I'm sure."

"That's what he said." I twirl my purple gel pen between my fingers.

"You're not buying it?"

"I don't know. He had this really weird look on his face. I can't explain it. I want to believe him, but as you know, I have trust issues."

"Right. How could I forget the whole Stephanie episode?" He's referring to the time when I convinced myself Jonathan was cheating on me with his lawyer. It was a fuss over nothing; they're just friends. I tend to make up stories in my head. It's one of the side effects of being a writer.

"Listen, pussycat. I wouldn't worry too much about it. There are far worse things in life," he says, his expression sullen. He's right. I should show some compassion for Jonathan's problem … whatever it is. "Just keep doing your thing and focus on the big picture, all right? Like making a major impact in Shanghai. We're all rooting for you, babe. I sure wish I could take off for Asia. I could use a break from being overworked and in the red."

"I wish I could take you with me. Maybe I could squeeze you into my luggage?"

We both laugh at how ridiculous that mental image is. The laughter seems to lighten up Jake a little.

"So … have you planned your travel wardrobe? How many dresses are you gonna bring for the fancy events?" He stares at me over the rims of his glasses for effect.

"Dresses?" I don't own any formal wear other than the dress made for me last semester by Ellie, a classmate who's in France right now. "I'll do like Cate Blanchett at Cannes and wear Ellie's dress over and over. It's the eco-responsible thing to do."

"Come on, Clem, you can do better than that. Lemme think of something. I have some ideas." He gives me a curious look. I don't think he gets that I really mean it when I say I want to reuse and recycle, but that's okay. I don't want to force my agenda on him.

"This is Shanghai we're talking about here! You need something bold and grand that makes a major statement! I want to see you in sequins, bows, bright colours!"

I mentally roll my eyes. He's overdoing it a bit. A formal evening gown, like life, can easily get overworked with too many frills. I'm in the mood for a minimalist, laid-back, serene vibe at the moment.

But for some reason, I doubt that's possible.

Chapter Five

"HELLO THERE, HANDSOME! You look like royalty," I say to Jake when we meet at our seats in the Broadhurst Theatre. I'm so excited to be here. I've heard nothing but good things about *Anastasia*, the Broadway show about the daughter of Tsar Nicholas II. The reviews have been great, and apparently the costumes are dreamy: stunning dresses made with hundreds of jewels and yards of silk, and a sixteen-karat gold crown. I can tell Jake is in heaven and, frankly, so am I.

He's really dressed up for tonight. He's wearing a pin-striped suit, a blue shirt, and a pink bowtie. The outfit is topped off with a fedora. He looks like a well-dressed jazzman about to play Lincoln Center. The look is Harlem suave meets Parsons flair, and it suits him perfectly.

"I'm so proud to be your date." I made an effort, too, and borrowed a black lace dress from Maddie's closet. It's one of the perks of living with a Parsons teacher who happens to be super fashionable.

"Right back at ya, Mademoiselle Bonjour." He holds up his rolled-up show program to one eye like a telescope and nods approvingly. "I'm happy you're here with me, Clem." He lays his hand on mine. "It means a lot."

"I wouldn't miss it for the world, if only to see you drooling over all those sequins."

We're both so passionate about fashion that we come to the theatre mostly to admire the costumes. Usually it's with rush or discounted tickets, but tonight, thanks to Jake's godmother, we're blissfully sitting in the second row. We're going to have an incredible view.

I've read that the costumes for this show are designed by Michelle Wong. Maybe I could interview her for *Bonjour Girl*. It's not exactly what Brian suggested, but it might satisfy him. It would be fascinating to find out more about a Tony Award–winning costume designer, especially her creative process and her inspiration.

Moments later, the curtain rises, and taffeta and rhinestones and an ocean of bright silk shimmer across the stage.

The music, the singing, the dancing, and the setting of Imperial Russia all transport me to a magical place. Jake could have invited his Russian blogger friend, Adelina, but chose me instead. This makes me feel even more warmly toward him.

The show is also distracting me from the fact that I'll be off to Asia in just a few weeks, which I'm sure was intentional on Jake's part. I've been feeling anxious about so many things:

1. Heading off to a new school — again.
2. Making new friends.
3. Interacting with relatives I haven't seen in ages.

4. The possibility of being bullied — again. I've been on guard ever since it happened, as if bullies lurk behind every corner.
5. Leaving behind two of my favourite people: Jonathan and Jake, my two J's. They're my rock, my safe harbour, and in Jake's case, my comic relief.

I've been reminding myself that it's only a summer; the program will be over before I know it. And the experience will be great for my career as a fashion journalist and super inspiring for my blog, too.

I should be excited about going to Shanghai. The fashion scene is huge in China right now. In addition to being a major manufacturing centre for the industry, China is a nation of passionate fashion followers and people who want to be a force in designing it, too. Shanghai Fashion Week is gaining success, and Chinese designers are taking the world by storm.

I follow countless inspirational Chinese bloggers who are documenting all of the above, including Gogoboi, Leaf Greener, and Mr. Bags. I, too, want to participate in the conversation about the evolution of Chinese fashion and be at the forefront of the discussion on Chinese eco-fashion. Based on Henry's Instagram page, there are lots of events in China relating to this issue right now. I can't wait to be a part of it all.

As the dancers and singers sashay across the stage and the first act comes to an end, I look over at my best friend — he's completely enthralled by the spectacle. He fans himself with his show program, holding it like a paper fan. I smile, wishing again that he could tag along on my trip. But I'm sure he'll get there some other time. We'll go together one day to promote his collection. A girl can dream. In the meantime, I'm going to take in this special moment; once again, I'm in the right place, at the right time.

"How about we grab some dim sum?" Jake says after we exit the theatre. "It'll get you in the mood for Shanghai, and we can catch up."

"That sounds great." I can always count on Jake when it comes to having fun and finding the best food. After fashion, those are his greatest passions.

"Can you cover me for dinner, though, Clem? I'm a bit short on that front."

"Sure, don't worry about it. It's my treat — you invited me to the show."

I'm on a high from seeing all that beauty and talent tonight. During the intermission, I even sent an email to Michelle Wong through her website, at Jake's urging.

"I'll look up the closest dim sum place," he says, pulling out his phone. He hands me his matching umbrella and raincoat, his large leather man bag, and his silk scarf. I stumble a bit loaded with his heavy gear, which smells like his sweet cologne, and give him a look. He lifts his shoulders and shoots me a sheepish grin.

He taps on his phone, and seconds later, his face lights up.

"All right, we're in luck! I found a cool place a few blocks away. The theatre district is full of dim sum. Let's go, I'm starving."

The restaurant is on the fifth floor of a walk-up on 49th Street. The stairs creak under our feet. As soon as we reach the top, a young Chinese woman ushers us inside and seats us at a large, round table next to some other diners. I love this kind of place; the vibe is so welcoming, and it reminds me of the places my dad used to take me on Sundays back in Paris.

We sit next to a guy with a muscle shirt and a tween with purple hair and nails who's staring at her phone. Jake winks and I smile back. New York is so much fun. I'm going to miss moments like this when I'm in China.

After we order some tea, Jake zeroes in on me.

"So what are you worried about, anyway? Jonathan is crazy about you. And you'll have so much fun in Shanghai! Apparently the city is a blast, and there are so many great restaurants. I read about this place called —" he pulls out his phone to check "— Dao Jiang Hu. It's regional fusion, and *dao jiang hu* is an expression that means 'full of shit.' How hilarious is that? Take a look, it's decorated with vintage hair rollers!"

"That sounds like a scene out of *Hairspray*. Only you could find a place that cool. I'll make sure to drop by in your honour."

"Please do! I want pictures of you next to the wall of plastic hair rollers. That will be fabulous."

"Not sure I want to be seen next to a wall of plastic, though. That goes against the editorial values of *Bonjour Girl*."

"Oh, right," Jake says, staring down at his funny plastic phone cover. His cheeks turn red. Jake and I have realized that all the plastic trinkets we once found so entertaining are killing our planet fast.

"I was just being facetious, Jake. Everything in moderation, right?"

"Definitely," he says, calling the waiter over. He orders a cart full of dumplings. I begin to laugh. So much for *that*.

"So, you have editorial values? That's impressive ... and intense."

"Yep. Blogger ethics are a thing, you know. I don't promote anything that's plastic or really harmful to the environment. That's part of my guidelines."

"Don't be too rigid with those guidelines, though, Clem. Remember, Brian suggested we think outside the box ... "

"I know he wants me to expand and be more visible and commercial, but that's not really me. I *am* willing to try new things, though. Interviewing Michelle Wong will be my first attempt at something a little different. She's an artist and businesswoman."

"That's an interesting angle, but I'm sorry to burst your bubble, hon — that ain't exactly thinking outside the box. Try to add some shock value to your post or something."

"Like what?"

"I dunno. Maybe talk about affairs between Broadway performers, or some behind-the-scenes scandal?"

I throw my napkin at him. "Totally off topic!"

"M'kay, if you say so. You're clever, you'll think of something cutting edge ..."

The way he says this fills me with self-doubt, and also, I'm annoyed. My blog is doing well as it is, so why does everybody have an opinion on how I could change it? But I bite my tongue. I know Jake has only good intentions.

"What about you? Any ideas for your collection?"

"Yeah. My mom and I talked about it the other day, and we came up with a cool new concept," he whispers, looking around to make sure no one can overhear. "Dress shirts and dresses with magnetic buttons for people with arthritis."

"What a great idea! Love it."

"Thanks. I just can't see when I'll have time to execute it, though, not to mention the costs. Things are crazy right now," he says, sounding a bit discouraged.

"Don't put too much pressure on yourself. You'll end up behaving like Jonathan."

"Oh? What do you mean?"

"He was really weird last night."

"Again? What happened?"

"I texted him and asked if we could talk. He said yes, then changed his mind and said he was too busy. I just don't get it. I'm starting to feel rejected."

"Hmm, weird. Did he tell you why?"

"No, not really. All I know is that it's work related. He said he would tell me later."

"That sounds intriguing. You just love a good mystery, dontcha?"

"Not really, but for some strange reason, they seem to find me."

Jake waves a server over and gets us a basket of steamed pork buns and some more tea.

"Come on, Clem, eat before it gets cold!" He reaches for another dumpling.

"You mean before you eat them all?"

"Yeah, that too."

I grab one, too, and we playfully bump our dumplings together. The muscle-shirt guy next to us gives us a disapproving stare. We giggle.

"Never mind about Jonathan. You're representing our school in Shanghai, and that's pretty major."

"I know. Lots of people are counting on me to impress, including Maddie. I just hope I can make everybody proud."

"Everybody's cheering for you. Of course there's lots of pressure to perform. I understand that. But you'll do well. You always do."

"Thanks. And thanks for bringing a dose of spontaneity into my life."

"That's why I'm here! To support your inner warrior, not the *worrier*. Now speaking of spontaneity, how about a nightcap at the Russian Tea Room?" he asks, his eyes gleaming with excitement.

"You mean right now? Pretty decadent for a school night …" I raise an eyebrow. But Maddie is still out of town, so no one is waiting for me at home. I guess it's doable.

"Are you in or are you out?" he asks impatiently.

"I say spontaneity wins. And so does a diva attitude."

"It takes one to know one."

I'm actually excited. I've always wanted to check out the Russian Tea Room. It's a landmark New York City restaurant on 57th Street. So many films and TV shows have filmed scenes there, including *Gossip Girl*. Plus, it'll be a fitting end to our Russian-themed night.

"But I'm staying away from vodka," I say. "We don't get along."

Jake lifts his cup of jasmine tea. "Whatever you want, tsarina. Your wish is my command."

The decor inside the Russian Tea Room takes my breath away. It's like walking into a scene from *Anastasia*. The main room is emerald green with dreamy red and gold chandeliers from which glass eggs are suspended. The way the light hits the glass creates a fairy-tale-like ambiance. Just like the Broadway show did, this space transports me to the magnificence of Imperial Russia.

There are impressive paintings on the walls and antique gold urns everywhere, adding a touch of baroque to this grandiose space. I imagine celebrities and social-ites sitting on the red banquettes, munching on toast and caviar, while business deals take place at the more secluded tables.

I've read that fashion designer Diane von Furstenberg enjoys this place. I can picture her coming here for business lunches.

Jake nods for me to follow him to the bar. He waves the server over and orders a martini for himself, sparkling water for me. The last time I drank vodka, I ended up pole dancing in front of strangers in a nightclub downtown and passing out in my boyfriend's apartment. Not the most mature behaviour. In fact, it was downright embarrassing. It took me weeks to get over it. I still cringe when I think about it. I lay my credit card on the bar.

Jake gives me a grateful nod. "Thanks, Clem."

I take a sip of my drink and smile, noticing how at ease my best friend looks in this grand place.

"So, are you feeling better, love? Not so anxious anymore?"

"Definitely. I always feel better when we spend time together. What will I do without you in China?" I reach over and rub his shoulder.

"That, my dear, is a good question." He takes a sip of his martini, then removes an olive with his fingers and pops it into his mouth. "You can always FaceTime me. I'll still be there for you, babe. I want you to leave for Shanghai feeling relaxed, not a nervous wreck. No more of that insecurity stuff, okay?"

"Yes, sir." I give him the peace symbol, showing off my cherry-red manicure.

Jake's phone rings and his eyes bulge when he sees the number on the screen. A look of panic comes over his face. "All righty," he says, "let's get the hell outta here." He grabs my arm and yanks me toward the door.

"What happened? Is something wrong?" This scene feels like déjà vu from a few nights ago with Jonathan.

"Nope. It's a school night, love. Time for bed. Let me help you get a cab so you can get home safely." He's nearly sprinting toward the door, dragging me along by my arm.

As soon as we exit the building, Jake waves down a yellow cab. He's not in the mood to chat — far from it. He just wants to send me off. I give him a warm hug and a peck on the cheek, then slip into the cab's back seat.

Now I have two mysteries to crack. But I'll get to the bottom of it. I always do.

After brushing my teeth and changing into my PJs, I check my phone and see that I have a message from Henry on Instagram. He's sent me some informational materials about the fashion school in Shanghai. I smile. I'm so lucky to have met someone who's been studying at the Condé

Nast Center of Fashion & Design for over a year already and is super knowledgeable.

My heart leaps when I see that I also have a text from Jonathan — then sinks when I start reading it.

> Hi sweetie, I'm so sorry for not call-
> ing you. Things have been a bit crazy
> ever since I got back from Italy, and an
> unexpected issue has come up. I can't
> really tell you about it yet — there are
> legal issues involved — except to say
> that something major is going down and
> it needs all of my attention. It breaks
> my heart that I can't share this with you
> right now, because I sure could use your
> big-hearted presence. I'm a frickin wreck.
>
> Please know that you're always on my
> mind. I'll call you in the next few days to
> explain. Please send me good vibes. I
> need them badly.
>
> Love you, XOXO

Now I'm really worried. What is going on? Was Jonathan arrested or something? Is he in jail? My mind goes into overdrive. I text him, but get no reply. This fantastic evening just took a really dark turn. I start to brew some hot cocoa. While I wait, I wrap a blanket around my shoulders and try not to chew on my nails.

An old Jack Johnson song that Maddie likes, "Sitting, Waiting, Wishing," plays in the back of my mind. No one said waiting on love was easy. Sometimes it can be downright brutal.

Chapter Six

"THANKS AGAIN FOR the fabulous night out last week. The show was spectacular, and thanks to you, I've scored an interview with Michelle Wong, one of the greatest costume designers in New York!" I lift my cup of tea to toast Jake.

He takes a large swig of coffee and responds with a grin. It looks a bit forced to me, though. It must have something to do with our mysterious exit from the Russian Tea Room. I won't mention it. I hardly slept last night and want to avoid any difficult conversations today.

The school café is buzzing with activity. We're getting close to crunch time; the semester ends in a couple of weeks. Students are putting in extra hours to keep their heads above water.

"All I did was encourage you to email her. You and your blog speak for yourselves, love, with great writing and killer topics. And quality over quantity. That's what truly matters. I'm sure that's why Michelle agreed to meet you."

"Well, I couldn't do it without your support. I still get this insecure feeling every time I'm about to publish something online, like Stella's waiting in the shadows of the internet to attack me." Stella was the student who was bullying me last semester. I still feel the sting of some of her comments.

"But you'll get over it. And anyway, the school warned her about harassing you again, didn't they?"

"Yup. The dean said their lawyers sent her a letter."

"Then keep that in mind. Believe in yourself. Everything else is just noise in your head," he says, as though he's giving himself that advice, too.

I redirect my attention to Jake's outfit. He's wearing red jeans, a bright-blue vest, a *We Are All Feminists* T-shirt, and rainbow-coloured Converse sneakers.

"Nice shirt."

"Thanks. I wear it in support of you and all of my lady friends."

"Much appreciated. Speaking of support, how are the new pieces for your collection coming along?"

"Working nights and weekends again to get a few more pieces created. But it's hard to focus when the money is tight. What I need most is cash to pay my bills."

"I hear you." I wish I could do something for him, but what? All I can do is change the subject. "I checked my numbers this morning. I have a few hundred more followers since last month, and readership is up. That interview with Michelle Wong should get some attention. I'm really psyched about meeting her."

"I bet. And you'll get plenty more attention in Shanghai. I'm sure there are people from that exchange program following you already," he says, winking.

How did he sense that I *do* have a mysterious, attractive follower in Shanghai? Actually, I'm dying to tell him all about Henry. After all, Jake is my confidant and he knows everything about me. A little gossip can't hurt.

"As a matter of fact —"

But before I can finish, Jake retrieves his buzzing cellphone from his bag. "Oh shit! Not again … Sorry, Clem, I gotta go!" He jumps from his seat, picks up his papers in record speed, tosses his half-eaten smoked salmon bagel in his bag, and runs out the door.

Once again, I've been abandoned by a man mid-meal. I'm starting to wonder if it's me or some kind of curse. But as I take a sip of tea, I remind myself that I'm not the cause of Jake's or Jonathan's weird behaviours or woes. Whatever is happening in their lives is their business. So why do I feel responsible? That's just ridiculous.

Maybe it's a good thing I'm heading off to Shanghai after all.

Chapter Seven

I'VE AGREED TO MEET Michelle Wong at the New-York Historical Society, an American history museum located at the corner of 77th Street and Central Park West. I decided to leave home early so I could plan how to tackle the interview while taking a leisurely walk through Central Park.

Walking past the majestic Gucci store on Fifth Avenue, I notice photos in the window of Gucci's year of the dog collection, a light-hearted collaboration with a renowned artist inspired by Chinese astrology. I read in a magazine that the two Boston terriers whose likenesses are emblazoned on the collection's bags, sneakers, jackets, and cardigans are the beloved pets of Gucci's creative director. The style is playful, with pops of bright red, pink, and purple, floral skirts, and big, baggy cardigans, but in my humble opinion, the bags painted with dogs' faces look a little DIY.

Jake thinks it's a lazy and over-the-top marketing ploy to appeal to the Chinese market. I wonder if the fact that his application for an internship at Gucci was turned down has anything to do with his opinions. But in any case, I think he's right.

I recently came across another label's year of the dog–inspired shirt that was covered in horrific-looking poodles, as well as a gold makeup compact encrusted with diamonds in the shape of a dog produced by one of the largest cosmetics companies in the world. Same idea, same questionable taste.

It's surprising how these brands have little to no understanding of what appeals to Chinese consumers of high-end fashion. Why don't they conduct better cultural research, or hire local designers? The dog theme that so many jumped on that year was such a vague connection to the Chinese market that it felt patronizing and out of touch.

Also, the use of girly, sweet-looking Asian models in the campaign photos is pretty stereotypical. I would have preferred to see someone like Chris Lee, the singer who rose to fame after winning the Chinese singing contest *Super Girl* — think *American Idol* meets *The Voice*, but on a much grander scale. Her look is androgynous and cutting edge.

One of the male models reminds me of my new Instagram friend, Henry. I wonder what he thinks of this collection? And what would Jonathan think of it? Would he think it's kitschy? I'll have to ask him about it when he resurfaces from whatever's going on with him.

I take some pictures on my phone of the satin bomber jacket in the window. Chinese astrology–inspired fashion would be a great subject for a *Bonjour Girl* article. That would make for out-of-the-box reading material, no?

Despite the questionable dog collection, Gucci's gorgeous store windows and the beautiful clothes inside restore my faith in my chosen path. I'm grateful to have the chance to study under some of the greatest fashion minds on the planet and alongside some of the best new talents. I shouldn't question my teachers' suggestions. They have far more experience than I do. They surely know best.

I need to be dog loyal to my mentors, and to my friends. No wallowing in insecurity or doubt. Jonathan and Jake are two of the city's most adorable creatures and more than worthy of my attention and admiration, but they sure aren't making things easy for me.

The New-York Historical Society was founded in 1804 as New York's first museum and has terrific exhibits about the city and American history. The building is magnificent, a gem overlooking Central Park. I'm glad I got here early, so I can take a good look around and be thoroughly prepared. Standing in this elegant, storied building transports me to another era. I guess it's only fitting, since we'll be talking about a different era, namely Imperial Russia.

The museum's restaurant, Storica, is a bright, spacious room with cheery yellow banquettes and big gold chandeliers, reminding me of the gold tiara worn by the female lead in *Anastasia*.

Michelle Wong will be the first major public figure I interview for *Bonjour Girl*. I order some chai and biscotti while I mentally rehearse the questions I've prepared. Of course, I want to know about her creative process and about *Anastasia*, but what I'm most interested in is how she started out, how she came to design costumes for opera, dance, and theatre, and how she worked her way to the top, eventually winning a Tony and other prestigious awards.

I'm also curious to learn what challenges and disappointments she's faced, and how she overcame them.

I've gone all out for this special interview: I'm wearing a vintage tea dress with giant red roses on it, along with a black patent leather belt and matching Mary Janes. It's a dress Maddie and I found at the local flea market in Brooklyn. My small cross-body bag has the tarot symbol of the wheel of fortune on its front. I hope it brings me good vibes — I sure could use some right now; I'm feeling nervous.

But the text I get from Jake lifts my spirits.

Good luck with the interview! Not that
you need luck. Just be your fabulous
self and knock her socks off. Mwah, big
hugs, XOXO

I look up from my chai to see Michelle Wong walking in. I can tell just from her demeanor that she's a dynamo. She's petite and confident looking in a beautiful blue silk circle skirt and jacket and light-yellow sweater underneath. She's elegant with a no-nonsense sensibility.

"Hello, Clementine," she says, graciously shaking my hand and taking her seat. "So sorry I'm a bit late. I had a meeting downtown and got stuck on the train." I'm amazed that she crossed Manhattan at rush hour to meet me. This gives me a major confidence boost.

"No worries at all, I understand. I've just been enjoying this divine museum. It's a great meeting place. Thank you for suggesting it."

Michelle orders some tea for herself, then I pull out my notebook and begin asking away. The truth is that I'm so passionate about this stuff that I really don't need any notes. I'm just following my heart.

"So, that red dress Anya wears in the finale! Can we talk about that?" I ask. I'm talking about a show-stopping crimson gown worn by the female lead in *Anastasia*. I could barely contain myself, looking at it during the show. "I almost cried when I saw her in it." I must have stars in my eyes right now. "And my date did, too."

She smiles. "You're not the only one. The actress wept the first time she tried it on."

"I bet she did. Red makes such a bold statement. Especially with all those jewels."

"The red, of course, is very Russian," Michelle says, "and the decoration on the front of her bodice is reminiscent of the imperial family's crest."

I scribble notes furiously. "And that amazing silhouette?"

"The silhouette just came from my imagination. The skirt is more of a 1950s silhouette. Just like the dress you're wearing," she says approvingly. The fact that she noticed my dress makes me giddy. I'm so happy I made the effort.

"Yes, I love all the different influences. What was your design process?" I ask, as the server brings more tea.

"For this show, I turned to paintings and photographs, including the photos Tsar Nicholas II took of his own family. I also looked through museum catalogues. Once I finish my research, I start sketching. Each sketch takes about an hour to draw and paint."

"And the fabrics?" I know this is the type of information Jake would want to know. He's obsessed with fabrics and he'd kill me if I didn't ask.

"I prefer to pick fabrics for the entire show at once — I never design one gown on its own — so I require thousands of swatches to choose from. It's quite a process."

"Wow, I wish I could be a fly on your wall and watch you pick all those swatches!"

"Oh no, you don't. It gets pretty messy."

My own writing process can get messy at times, too. I'll cut out inspiring articles from magazines and place them randomly over the floor in my room; then I'll have all kinds of ideas buzzing around in my head until everything comes together on the page.

By the time I've finished my biscotti and the last dregs of my tea, we've finally come to the questions I've been dying to ask since she got here.

"So how did you do it? How did you get to where you are today?"

"There's no secret formula, Clementine. I did it thanks to tons and tons of hard work. I've worked on over five hundred shows, large and small, and not always the most glamorous. But no matter what I was doing, I showed up with the same work ethic, always."

"Any major challenges you'd like to share? Any particular blunders?"

"Oh god, way too many to talk about! I've seen it all. I've been on the verge of creative catastrophe many times, like the time my costumes were delivered to the wrong theatre, so they arrived late, or the time a lead actor couldn't fit into his costume after gaining some weight. I'll just say that there's a solution to every problem, Clementine, no matter what it is. There's nothing you can't overcome, no matter how dramatic or painful. I'm speaking from experience." She finishes her tea in one gulp.

This is the kind of advice I love to share with my readers and, more importantly, with myself. I can tell that she's had to work hard to get where she is and to fight her way to the top.

"Has it been challenging, as a woman, to establish yourself in the industry?"

Michelle stares into her empty cup for a moment, then looks up. Her eyes meet mine. "There have been ups and downs. People who have treated me with respect and people who have made things difficult for me, whether consciously or not," she says carefully. "Sometimes being a woman means that you constantly have to prove yourself to your superiors, even where other colleagues don't have to, and even though it isn't fair. But, if you're passionate about what you do and good at it, Clementine, no one can touch you. Being a strong, determined woman is a good thing."

"I read online about the ballet you worked on that toured through China. I'm actually leaving soon for an exchange program in Shanghai. Do you have any recommendations for me?"

"If you like theatre, you might want to check out a Beijing opera at the Yifu Theatre."

"Cool, I'll make sure to check it out."

"The theatre's quite romantic, a great place for a date," she says with a smirk. I blush, thinking of Henry. Why can't I stop thinking about him?

"Thank you for sharing all of this with me, Michelle. This was an immense honour."

"Don't mention it. It was a pleasure. Good luck in Shanghai. I'm sure you'll have a blast!" She gives me a playful grin. She's genuine, keen, and endearing — the kind of woman who belongs on *Bonjour Girl*.

As soon as I get home after class, I change into some comfy lounge pants and a baggy T-shirt and brew myself a pot of jasmine tea. I'm grateful to have the apartment to myself. The place is quiet — ideal conditions to write a kick-ass blog post. I light a scented candle, inhale its refreshing aroma, and begin typing away.

All through class this afternoon, I was replaying my conversation with Michelle. Her advice and her get-it-done mentality really gave me the boost I needed.

I type up the article, sharing some of Michelle's inspirational advice. With permission, I add pictures of some of the gorgeous dresses and impressive jewels she designed for *Anastasia*, names of stores in New York where she sources her fabrics, along with links (mostly as a hot tip for Jake, but also as a tentative step toward Brian's suggestion), and a list of her favourite designers (also linking to their online stores). I also share a selfie of me and Michelle we took at the museum.

I've got the *Anastasia* soundtrack playing on my computer to provide me with positive energy as I write. Thanks to the music and to Michelle's wise words, I'm excited to press *publish*.

Once I've shared my post, I check my phone.

I have a new message on Instagram. It's from Henry.

Hey, Clementine, thought you'd
like this. It's from a cool designer in
Shanghai. It's 100 percent recycled
fabric.

It's a picture of a jean jacket that's been dyed and adorned with patches of moons and stars.

Yes, thanks! I love it! So unique!

Like you!

My fingers freeze. I don't know how to respond. It takes me a minute to figure out a comeback that won't sound flirtatious.

😊 Thanks! I do my best but it's not
always easy. Sometimes people
try to steer me in different directions
that aren't totally me ...

Really? Who? And more importantly,
why?

Not sure. One of my teachers told
me I need to think outside the box —
expand my horizons in my blog

You already do! What about all those
interviews of teens with disabilities and
life challenges last semester? I mean

that's totally unique … You are one of
a kind! Don't let anyone convince you
otherwise, okay?

Thanks for the pep talk, Henry. It's
coming at the right time. And thank you
for supporting my blog!

My pleasure! I was going to type "that's
what friends are for" but I don't want to
be too presumptuous …

We can be friends, I'd like that …
Thanks for your support, friend

I'd like that too 😊

TTYL!

Chapter Eight

I WAKE UP THE NEXT morning to an email from Michelle Wong that makes my heart flutter. She read my blog post after I tagged her on social media last night, and she shared the interview immediately with all her friends.

> What a terrific article, Clementine. I'm
> impressed with your writing, and I love
> the playful tone of your article, too.
> Keep up the great work and have fun in
> Shanghai!

I jump out of bed and forward Michelle's message to Jake. Within seconds, he texts:

> Way to go Clem! You rock! Off to read
> the interview. Talk to you later, you
> BADASS babe.

I take a look at my blog traffic on Google Analytics — it's through the roof. I have hundreds of retweets, thanks to my own readers and Michelle's friends. I sigh with relief.

My post may not have been that out of the box, according to Jake's standards, but my readers seem to appreciate it, and that's what matters most.

Ecstatic, I jump in the shower and wash my hair with my organic rose shampoo, and by the time I get out, I'm flying, light as a hummingbird. I'm super grateful for Brian and Jake's feedback, but the truth is, I'm free to write about whomever and whatever I want. While I'm towelling myself off, I finally get a text from Jonathan asking if I want to get together for coffee tomorrow. I sigh with relief again. So far, this is a really good day.

My elation continues during the train ride to school, as I glue my eyes to my phone, watching for more views and mentions. There are lots more — but I remind myself that I'm not doing this for the attention. If my content inspires my readers, then I'm happy. One thing's for sure: Michelle inspired *me*, and for that I'm grateful.

As soon as I arrive at Parsons, I head down to the school cafeteria, looking for Jake at our usual meeting spot. When I don't see him, I take a seat in the corner with a cup of tea. As I bask in the glory of Michelle's compliment about my blog post, I notice a few students looking at me, some smiling or nodding. I guess Michelle's inspiring message has reached them, too.

I'm soaking in all the feel-good energy when Brian walks over with a big smile.

"Hey, Clementine! Way to go with the blog!" he says, holding his morning coffee. "It's a great start to branching out! Keep up the great work, okay?"

"Thanks, Brian, that means a lot. And thanks for your support."

After Brian leaves, I see James Williams paying for his breakfast. He's the dean of the school, as well as my cousin Maddie's boyfriend. He waves at me and comes over. It looks like I'm on a roll.

"Hey, Clementine, great job on the interview," James says loudly. To my surprise, he leans over and offers his hand for me to shake, which I do. "Maddie forwarded it to me this morning. This is why we selected you to go to Shanghai."

"Oh, thank you, James. I appreciate the feedback."

I'm not sure it was a good idea for James to say this publicly. I know he means that my writing was the reason they nominated me for the exchange program, but I'm worried people might think I was favoured because of our personal connection. I'm really sensitive to this stuff, especially after what happened last semester.

"One day, you'll be covering fashion for the *New York Times*, I'm sure of it!" As he walks away, I notice some students at a nearby table staring at me. This sends shivers down my spine.

And just like that, all of my joy comes crashing down. Last semester, Stella unfairly accused me of receiving privileges because of my relation to Maddie. Even though the school dealt with her, I'm still worried and self-conscious about whether others believe that I don't deserve to be here. Will this awful feeling ever go away?

But what would Michelle Wong advise me to do? Probably to lift my head high and ignore my imagined detractors. My blog post was popular with my readers, two faculty members liked it, and Michelle herself appreciated it. Her words gave my self-esteem a serious boost.

But the truth is, I'm still feeling a bit unsteady inside.

Between classes, I spot Jake in one of the hallways, leaning against a wall and texting. He's looking sharp in a grey blazer and Mello Yello vintage T-shirt accessorized with eyeglasses made from a repurposed vinyl record. He got them as a gift. They're from a brand called Vinylize. It totally works on him; he looks supremely cool.

I wish I could say the same for myself. I'm sweating just thinking about the way those students stared at me in the café.

As I approach, Jake throws his phone into his saddle-bag as though he doesn't want me to glimpse who he's texting. Does this have anything to do with his mysterious exit from the Russian Tea Room and from the school café?

"Great post, Clem. I really enjoyed it," he says a bit flatly. Does his tone reflect his true opinion of the blog post, or is it related to the texts he was just looking at? It's hard to tell.

"Do you have a minute?" I ask.

"Sure, babe. What's up?" Jake asks, looking concerned. "Is it about Jonathan?"

I shake my head. "No ... although I *am* worried about him. He's really stressed out but still hasn't told me what the deal is."

"So what's going on?"

I take a deep breath and exhale slowly, looking around to make sure no one's listening.

"I'm worried about a conversation I had with the dean earlier."

"Oh, what about?" he whispers.

"He complimented me on the interview, which was great, but he also mentioned Maddie and said something about Shanghai. Some students from our class were sitting right next to me, and after he left, they were staring at me, so now I'm worried they think I was picked for Shanghai because my cousin is dating the dean or something."

Jake stares at me incredulously. "You wanna know what I think? You're just being paranoid and you need to cut it out. Who cares about what other students think? You're using this fear of bullying as an excuse to stay stuck, backpedal your way out of going to China, and not move forward with your life. You need to develop a backbone and just move the fuck on."

Ouch.

I stand there with my hands on my hips, my mouth hanging open, unable to find the words to respond. I was expecting him to just lend a sympathetic ear, but he's clearly not in the mood for it.

Sometimes the truth hurts, and you need to swallow it. Am I stuck on what other people think of me? Probably. What am I so afraid of? Being seen for who I am? Succeeding on an international scale?

But that's what bullying does to you. It plays tricks with your mind and leaves deep scars, keeps you stuck in fear, questioning your every move, dragging yourself along as though walking through cement.

Instead of arguing with Jake, I decide to follow his advice and just drop it. Literally. I throw my empty cup in the recycling bin and walk toward the elevators.

"Clem, wait! Where are you going?" he asks, looking flustered. "I didn't mean to say it like that. Come back!"

"No, no, you're absolutely right. I'm moving on. So please excuse me while I go to find my backbone," I say with a hint of sarcasm as the elevator doors close.

I can just imagine the smirk of pride on his face. It mirrors mine.

Chapter Nine

"SO ARE YOU GOING to tell me what's going on?" I ask Jonathan. "I've been really worried about you." We're at Joe Coffee on 13th Street, our favourite hangout spot near Parsons, sitting side by side on stools facing the street. I haven't slept much since I got his mysterious message, but I'm feeling empowered by Jake's pep talk. No more hiding. I'm going to tell it like it is, at least for today. It's all about baby steps.

I found time between two afternoon classes to meet Jonathan. He's shooting some Parsons collections again today. I'm relieved to see him out and about.

He looks down into his cappuccino, nervously pulls his hand out of mine, and runs his fingers through his hair.

Instead of pressing for an answer, I back off and take a sip of my tea. I'm trying not to push, but I need him to tell me the truth. Even if it's difficult. I rub his back while we watch students walking down the busy sidewalk. The more I rub, the more he slumps forward. "Whatever it is, you can tell me," I say softly.

After a moment, he wraps his fingers around his ceramic mug, takes a long gulp of coffee, and finally turns to face me.

"All right." He takes a long, deep breath in, then sighs. "Something happened in Italy." He sighs again and looks away. "Something that could really hurt my business."

I feel a tight knot in the pit of my stomach. *Oh no*.

"I'm being subpoenaed to testify in a lawsuit," he blurts out.

"What kind of lawsuit?" The pit in my stomach becomes a grapefruit, but I continue rubbing his back. My mind races. Is he in major trouble?

"I feel like total shit."

I place both my hands over his. I wish I could take his pain away. "How bad is it?"

"Pretty bad. Like this-could-kill-my-business kind of bad. The business I've worked so hard to build." He bites his lower lip. "You know me, Clem, I don't come from money. I've worked myself to the bone for everything I've got. It was so hard for me to be taken seriously as a young photographer. Now all that could be for nothing."

Has he gotten caught up in some kind of fraud? Money laundering or theft? Surely not. Jonathan is a super honest man and would never do anything like that.

"Come on, Jonathan, just tell me, please!"

After looking everywhere but my direction, he finally turns to me, his eyes filled with tears. "Sexual harassment."

It can't be. "What? What are you talking about?"

He rushes to explain, seeing the alarm on my face. "No, don't worry, *I* didn't harass anyone — that's not what this is about."

My gut unclenches just a little. "Then what?"

He sighs. "One of my biggest clients was arrested for sexual harassment and assault." He lets his face fall into his hands. "I just can't believe I'm being dragged into this."

"What happened?"

"An assistant claims my client harassed her after a photo shoot, then attacked her. The prosecution is calling me in as a character witness against him. I didn't witness this attack, but I know he has a bad reputation and he can be slimy around women. *That* I've seen before. But if I testify against him, I'll lose his business and who knows how many other important clients. I want to do what's right … but I'm scared."

Jonathan has impeccable ethics and a solid character — that's why he gets to work with such a prestigious client as Parsons. I understand that this is not an ideal situation, but I know he'll survive it.

"But you're doing the right thing. Hopefully, you'll help put a stop to this predator. You're in good hands with Stephanie. And I'm here for you, too."

"But also you're leaving for Shanghai in a couple of weeks, Clem. I wish I could spend time with you instead of dealing with all this. What horrible fucking timing." He holds my hand tightly.

I reach up and touch his cheek. "It doesn't matter. We'll get through this, okay? You're resilient, and so am I."

But I can sense his concern about the distance that may come between us. Will we overcome this?

Chapter Ten

I CAN'T SLEEP. I've been tossing and turning all night. Jonathan's subpoena, his fears for his business, Jake's mood swings, Shanghai — it's all a bit too much to handle. I decide to get out of bed.

When all hell breaks loose around you, stay calm and remain focused on your passions and priorities. This will get you through the toughest of times. At least, that's what I tell myself.

I turn on my computer and try to think of blog ideas for *Bonjour Girl*. As much as I would love to help Jonathan and Jake, I can't just fix things for them. All I can do is lend an ear and offer some ideas. There's no magic wand to make other people's problems disappear.

Focusing on my own projects will help me get my mind off things I can't control. I'm sure that's what my great-grandmother Cécile would advise. I can't recall anything specific about helping friends through major crises in the etiquette book I inherited from her, but I'm sure she would say that even when a lady is providing moral support, she knows when to take a step back and focus on herself.

It'll be a struggle to concentrate on my writing right now, but it's the best way to go.

I'm scouring the internet to find a relevant topic to write about, when a notification pops up on my screen.

It's a message from Henry.

Maybe he's sending me more helpful information about our school and what classes I should take. Whatever it is, it'll be a welcome distraction, since I'm still having doubts about going to China.

His email says that he's in Hong Kong travelling at the moment, but he wanted to send me this surprise.

It's a link. I tap on it and it takes me to a YouTube video called *Dreaming of Shanghai*. The title image is a young woman holding a bunch of balloons, apparently floating over the Shanghai skyline, high above the famous Oriental Pearl Tower. It's ethereal — it reminds me of the first scene of the video I created for my Parsons portfolio way back. I tap *play*.

The video begins with a man's hand holding a paper fan decorated with pretty blue flowers. It lifts up to reveal a message handwritten in bright-blue ink: *Hello, dear Clementine!*

That's unexpected. It makes me smile.

The next sequence is in a park: a large group of seniors is practicing tai chi beside a giant weeping willow and a pond, moving in perfect synchrony. Their flowing movements are mesmerizing, so different from the daily hustle and bustle of New York. As they move in peaceful silence, the hand holds up another handwritten note, this time scribbled in bright-green ink, the same colour as the tree leaves: *Shanghai is ready to welcome you with open arms.* In the background, an elegant woman in the same group dressed in white linen opens her arms wide.

My eyes are glued to my computer screen. This could be an official video for the Shanghai tourism board. Except it's not — this was made just for me, to welcome me to the city.

The next sequence shows an outdoor market where a street vendor is selling lacquered boxes and other trinkets. A hand slowly opens one of the jewellery boxes. It's lined with red silk and contains a folded piece of paper. The hand lifts out the paper and unfolds it slowly, revealing a message in red ink: *Shanghai looks forward to receiving you and your precious gifts.*

The hand then opens the top of the box to reveal a secret compartment with a mirrored bottom, where another piece of paper lies folded. As two hands unfold the message, a tiny pearl rolls out. *The city welcomes your love of diversity … as it reflects our own jewels.*

The video is breathtaking. And I can't believe the effort Henry must have gone through to create it. I'm not sure what to make of this.

In another sequence, a message is hidden in a box of steaming dumplings picked up from a grinning street vendor: *We look forward to seeing more of your delicious sense of beauty and style.*

My mouth waters at the sight of the dumplings … and the messages are giving me a strange combination of feelings. I'm touched and hugely flattered, but also starting to feel mildly uncomfortable. Not to mention guilty.

The last sequence is in a fancy hotel. A valet opens the front door, and footsteps sound as the camera enters a grand lobby with large bouquets of flowers on antique furniture.

We go up a few flights of stairs, and then a hand turns a doorknob, opening the door that leads to a library filled with books, exquisite sofas, and side tables. On one of those tables is a dainty cup of tea, and next to it is a note. The hand unfolds the note slowly to reveal the last message, this one written in an elegant pink script: *We hope this city will open the door to your heart, just as you have captured ours.*

The video closes in on a bookcase. A pair of hands takes out the book *Shanghai Girls* by Lisa See and opens it to an underlined passage:

> Don't ever feel that you have to hide who
> you are. Nothing good ever comes from
> keeping secrets like that.

OMG. This is mindblowing, and he totally understands what I'm going through.

This video is so personal, so beautiful, so deeply touching. And yet we don't even know each other, really. It's so over-the-top that I should probably be creeped out by this level of attention from a strange man … and yet, somehow, I'm not. I just don't know how to respond. I mean, how *does* a girl respond to something like this?

I stare out the window, into the courtyard.

Could it be that we have a real connection, a special friendship, without ever having met? I feel a magnetic pull toward Henry — is that okay? Is it cheating emotionally?

Whatever it is, I'm putting it away safely in the lacquered jewellery box in my mind, until I find the right words with which to reply.

Chapter Eleven

THE ACTOR DENZEL WASHINGTON once said, "Ease is a greater threat to progress than hardship, so keep moving, keep growing, keep learning."

I'm thinking about that quote as I walk into the Parsons design studio looking for Jake. I know he's still in a bad place; he's been looking awfully depressed ever since his swift exit from the school café. But I also know he's far from being a quitter. So it's no surprise to find him hunched over a sewing machine, totally immersed in what he's doing. He's surrounded by other students, but doesn't seem to notice them, or me. He's wearing a pair of washed-out denim overalls, a white T-shirt, a silver-and-white baseball cap, and two pairs of eyeglasses — one is perched on top of his cap and the other is balanced on the tip of his nose.

He's sewing two pieces of delicate powder-blue silk into what looks like a long, ruffled skirt, the kind that fashion legend Oscar de la Renta would have created. The style of the skirt is quite different from Jake's usual, more minimalist style. Maybe this is his way of branching out creatively.

I can tell he's revelling in that sweet spot, the special place where an artist is fully engaged in his craft. I've been there. It feels like magic. I don't want to interrupt his momentum, so I decide to hang back for the time being. After a solid ten minutes of concentrated focus on the whirring machine, he looks up and sees me. He waves me over.

"Hey, Clem! Whatcha doin' over there?"

"Oh, just watching you create something divine. It's so inspiring to watch you work."

"Aw, thanks, Clemy. How do you like the skirt?" He removes his work of art from the machine and lifts it high above his head so I can see the details. "It's cocktail hour in Savannah meets torrid nights in Madrid." He has the same radiant smile that Michael Kors has when he salutes the crowd after a runway show.

"Jake, it's gorgeous! One of the new pieces?"

"Nope," he says, shaking his head. "It's a gift for my muse."

"Adelina! She'll love it." He's told me before that his friend Adelina, a Russian blogger, is his creative muse. It kind of made me jealous, to be honest.

"No, she wouldn't wear this. *C'est pour toi!*" he says with a flourish.

My jaw nearly hits the floor. I know how much time, energy, and money must have gone into this skirt. I wasn't expecting a gift from him, let alone such an extravagant one. Tears well up in my eyes.

"You made this for me? When did you have the time?"

"Oh, late at night when I couldn't sleep. It helped to get my mind off the bad stuff. It's for you to wear at one of those fancy schmancy galas in Shanghai."

"Thank you so much, Jake! I love it!" I give him a long, warm hug, then twirl around the room, holding the skirt up to my chest so that it doesn't touch the floor.

"Try it on and we'll get it fitted." He hands me the skirt, and I carefully pull it over my black leggings, then slide the leggings off underneath. I remove my bulky sweater, too. I can tell just from how the fabric feels and the way it cascades to the ground that it's going to look amazing.

Jake guides me to a long mirror and looks on proudly at his work. It looks great even with my simple white shirt.

"Don't forget to wear at least four-inch heels. Otherwise it'll drag on the floor and look like a mop," he instructs, kneeling down to show me the right length for the hem. I look down gratefully, and a question pops into my head: where should I first wear this skirt? New York or Shanghai?

While Jake crouches on the ground, pinning the final alterations, some of the other students get up from their workstations to take a closer look. My gaze wanders over to Jake's empty workstation. There appears to be some kind of card game open on his laptop screen; I can make out the words *Game Over* flashing. When I glance down at him, I see that he's caught me looking — he looks away quickly, his face crimson. I try to act like I haven't seen anything. Now is not the time to discuss it.

"Wow, Jake, you really outdid yourself," one male student says. He comes over to feel the exquisite fabric.

"Oh my god, it's stunning!" a female student says. Everyone in the studio looks on admiringly at his work. My friend truly has talent. He blushes and wipes away a tear. I know it's not a tear of joy, but hopefully all this praise will motivate him to press on, no matter what his obstacles or inner demons are.

"Friendship consists in forgetting what one gives and remembering what one receives." I love this quote by the French writer Alexandre Dumas. Jake has taught me about self-esteem and about trusting myself and, most importantly, about bringing more playfulness into my life. He's given me so much.

Today, it's my turn to bring some happiness his way.

"Thank you again for the gorgeous skirt, Jake. I still can't believe you made it for me. Especially when you're so swamped and stressed about work and school and money. I've never owned such a beautiful piece of clothing."

"Anything for you, babe." He smiles sadly.

We're sitting in our usual spot at the front of the room at Le Midi, a French brasserie and favourite hangout for Parsons teachers and students. It's a special place; I first met Jonathan here, and Jake and I come all the time to gossip, people-watch, catch up on life, and eat truffle fries.

"Is everything okay?" I'm hoping he'll open up to me, finally.

He just shrugs. He can't seem to sit still; he fidgets with his menu, nervously rifles through his bag for a few minutes, then awkwardly removes his glasses and looks off across the room. "I'm not hungry, Clem. I'll just watch you eat and have some water."

"Water?" I can tell things are bad, but I never imagined they were *this* bad. I've never heard anything so depressing as my gourmand friend, as passionate about food as he is about silk taffeta, ordering nothing but water. And he's just spent the last few hours working feverishly on my skirt, so he must be starving. "What do you mean you're not hungry?"

"I'm just not, that's all. Just let it be, okay?" He lifts his shoulders as if it can't be helped. "Besides, I need to lose weight." He looks sadder than ever.

"Oh, says who?"

"Me. That's who."

"Just stop it! You're perfect the way you are."

He scoffs. "Whatever. I'm far from perfect, that's for sure."

"Right." I wave the waitress over and proceed to order a burger, a salad, two orders of fries, and two iced teas, our usual lunch order. Jake shakes his head disapprovingly, but doesn't stop me. He seems distracted, lost in thought.

"So, listen, I know things are really tough," I say. "Do you want to tell me about it? Is it to do with your money problems?"

"What do you mean?"

"I'm not blind, Jake. You've been acting really strange. The way we left the Russian Tea Room all of a sudden, then running out of the school café that day. That was a poker website on your laptop, wasn't it? And now you're not eating? Don't just pretend everything's fine. Tell me what's up." He looks away. "You can trust me like a sister, Jake. You can tell me anything."

He looks around the room and wipes his face with his hand, then absentmindedly twists his napkin. "It's complicated, Clem. Really, really frickin' complicated."

"Okay, well I want to help you any way I can."

His eyes begin to water. Tears run down his cheeks. He lets his face fall into his hands and begins to sob. He's full-on crying, with fits of tears and sniffling and snorting. People next to us stare.

"I'm in deep trouble, Clem." He picks up his discarded eyeglasses and stares at them.

The two men in New York whom I care for the most — both in trouble at the same time.

"What kind of trouble?"

"The worst. Major financial crisis. I'm going down in flames." He makes an explosion noise.

"What happened?" I place a hand on his.

"Where do I begin?" He takes a breath and wipes his nose with his napkin. "I'm caught in a downward spiral to hell, that's what happened. Credit card debt, rent, expenses, and ..." His voice trails off. He looks out onto the street, down at his reading glasses, anywhere but at me. "And a massive gambling debt." He blows his nose hard. The woman sitting on the banquette next to us gives him a dirty look. He glares back at her, making her look away.

"Is it that bad?"

He nods. "It's really bad. Online poker. I got into it just for fun at first, as a distraction. Then I went to some clubs ... but I lost big time. I'm so ashamed." He rubs his eyes. I can tell he hasn't gotten much sleep lately; he's got dark circles around his eyes the size of poker chips.

He shakes his head and lets out a long sigh. "I may have to drop out of school to get a full-time job."

"No!" I can't believe what I'm hearing. It's far worse than I thought. The idea of losing Jake as a classmate makes me want to cry. All his incredible talent gone to waste.

"I'm so sorry, Jake. Why didn't you say something before? I could have tried to help you figure something out."

"It was easy money at first. It was great — my poker wins were helping to pay for stuff. Then I wanted to win more so I could expand my collection, hire a virtual assistant and a PR agency. That stuff's expensive. And I thought if I made bigger bets, I could win money more quickly ... but then I started losing. I racked up so much debt ... it's insane. I'm in deep trouble."

"Oh, Jake."

"That's not the worst of it," he says. "I started borrowing money from a loan shark. They charge crazy-high interest, too. Some of it I used to pay off debts. Some of it I gambled away again. I'm in the hole. They're nasty people, Clem. It's ... I'm scared."

"You mean scared for your life?" I say under my breath. I can't believe I'm asking this question.

"Something like that." He mimes shooting himself in the head along with a sound effect, and our seat neighbour stands to ask for the cheque. I can't say I blame her.

I'm just sitting there, slack-jawed.

I pray nothing bad happens to my friend and remember Michelle Wong's advice: there's a solution to every problem. There's nothing we can't overcome. We need to find a solution, fast. But what?

"How about selling a few pieces from your collection, or some skirts like the one you made me? I could help you. We could contact some high-end boutiques."

"Pfft. You think I haven't tried that? Do you know how many designers in New York City are trying to sell their stuff to boutiques? Or online? Way too many. Good luck!"

"All right, I get the picture, but you're not like everybody else, okay?"

"Whatever, Clem. Whatever." He's not in the mood or situation to take my compliment. I'd better drop it.

"So … what are these nasty people saying?" I ask.

"That they want to break my legs." Jake puts his glasses back on and smiles wryly.

"What?" I hope he's exaggerating.

"They've threatened to go after my parents' dry cleaning business if I don't pay them back. I don't know what to do. If my mom finds out, she'll be devastated."

As the waitress arrives with our food, an idea flashes through my mind — a plan. But I decide to keep it to myself for now; I'll need to think it through carefully before I say anything to Jake.

"All right," I say, picking up a fry, "for now, let's focus on the solution rather than the problem."

"Oh, man, Clem, you sound like a preacher." He eyes the plate of fries in front of him.

"I'm just repeating what you told me a couple of days ago, remember? It doesn't help to be negative. Not me, not you, and not Jonathan."

"What do you mean?"

I glance around the restaurant before whispering, "Jonathan's being called to testify as a witness in a nasty criminal case." I trust Jake with this information. And I really need to talk to someone about it.

"Oh god, what about?"

"His biggest client was arrested for sexual harassment and assault. He has to testify that he's witnessed similar behaviour, and he's really worried about it, because there's probably going to be some backlash against him."

"Oh man, that sucks. I'm so sorry to hear that. And I'm sorry I didn't even ask you how he's doing. I've been so caught up in my own bullshit."

"It's been rough on him," I admit. "He's barely slept in the last three days. He's a wreck. And it's sad that we can't be together more before I leave for the other side of the world."

"You guys will get through this. It's not like there's an actual problem between the two of you. It's just a bad situation."

I shrug. "I guess. Anyway, there's a temporary mood lifter sitting on that plate right in front of you."

He stares at the truffle fries, reaches for one, dips it in the rich mayo, and smiles. The contrast between his huge basket of fries and the *Eat More Kale* sweatshirt he was wearing a few days ago makes me burst out laughing. I explain it to him and he laughs, too.

Now we're getting somewhere. His mood has lightened up, so I guess now's a good time to mention Henry and his video. Before I even utter a word, though, my face turns bright red.

"You can tell me anything, Clem. You know that, right? I mean, I just shared my entire dark side with you. It wasn't easy," Jake says.

"Yes, I know ... I met this student from China. His name is Henry; he studies at the Condé Nast Fashion Center. We met on Instagram."

"Okay. That's nice. Is there something more I should know?"

"Well, he's been super friendly, sending me info about the school, but lately he's become flirtatious …"

"Oh, I see. Is he hot?"

I stare down into my plate of fries, blushing some more. I'm also a bit tongue-tied. "Yeah, he is."

"Oh boy. I smell danger ahead."

"The thing is, he sent me this video … and it's really beautiful and creative but a bit over-the-top and I'm just not quite sure what to make of it.…"

I pull out my phone and press *play*. After the video ends. Jake closes his eyes and smirks. "Oh man, Clem. You're in trouble."

Dear Henry, thank you for that beautiful video. It's AMAZING! I was speech-less! You're a talented storyteller and I can't wait to see more of your work in person. I'm really looking forward to discovering Shanghai after seeing all of those jaw-dropping scenes and that mouth-watering street food. And all that refinement you shared! Wow! Thanks again for being so thoughtful.

Your friend, Clem

I try to make my response sound friendly, especially after what Jake said at lunch. The last thing I need right now is any more trouble.

"Hey, babe, thanks a lot for stopping by before my next client gets here."

I'm at Jonathan's photography studio on the Lower East Side. It's an all-white space decorated very sparsely with a long, narrow wooden table, some mismatched chairs, a tiny kitchen, and an impressive shooting area complete with special lighting, reflective umbrellas, and large white screens.

He kisses me tenderly and takes my hand. He looks more rested today than he did the other day at Joe Coffee, although he still has dark circles under his eyes.

"Here, take a seat. Do you want something to drink?"

"No thanks. I just wanted to see how you were doing."

"I'm surviving. I'm just a witness, after all, I'm not the accused or the victim."

"Just surviving? That's a shame. With your talent and drive, you should be thriving."

He takes a seat across from me.

"I know. I'm just feeling rotten about it. I want to do what's right, but it's not going to be good for me."

I lay my hand on his. "Just with this one client, though."

"This client holds the decision-making power over a lot of projects I'm involved in."

"But what about *your* reputation … for honesty and ethics?"

He sighs, shakes his head, and crosses his arms. I can tell how worried he is about his business. This client pays most of the bills.

"You've seen him behaving inappropriately?" I ask.

"Not to that woman specifically, but to others, yeah. He's one of those men who think the world revolves around them and that they can do whatever they want, including assault women, and get away with it. He's narcissistic and controlling."

"He sounds disgusting."

"He is. And still, saying so under oath is going to cost me big time. I really can't afford to have this happen right now."

"You're resourceful. You'll find other clients. There are plenty of upstanding men and women in powerful positions, and they'll recognize your courage. You'll have proven your character. That means a lot."

He stares at me so long I'm wondering if he thinks I'm foolish or crazy, then he puts his hand on my cheek.

"Thank you."

"For what?"

"For being so brave when I'm such a chickenshit. And for reminding me that I'm being a greedy jerk."

"That's not what I said!"

"You're saying what I need to hear. Thanks for being you."

I smile and squeeze his hand.

"And thanks for being here," he says. "I tend to retreat from the world when things get tough. I've gotten used to figuring things out on my own. But talking to you has made me feel so much better."

"Don't retreat, especially not from me, okay? Promise you'll stop doing that."

"I promise." He grins, and I melt.

"Okay, good."

He stands up, pushes aside my bangs, and kisses my forehead.

"I want to show you the new account I set up on WeChat," I say, pulling out my phone. "It's a Chinese social media app you can use to follow me when I'm in Shanghai."

"Sounds great. I'll follow you anywhere, Clementine Liu."

He kisses me again, this time on the lips and with a lot more passion. I grab onto his sleeves and kiss him back, hard. His next client will be here any minute, so I hold on for as long as I can. I guess I'm the one being greedy now.

Chapter Twelve

"HEY, CLEMENTINE, I'M HOME!" Maddie's voice echoes throughout the apartment.

Maddie's been away on a mission to connect with another fashion school in Europe. Dean James Williams, her boyfriend, joined her in Paris for the weekend.

I run to greet her with a warm hug. I've missed her, especially her comforting presence and her amazing cooking. When she's not around, I just eat avocado toast or cold cereal. Both my heart and my stomach are grateful she's back.

I left school early this afternoon to clean up the apartment. I've been hard at work removing the clutter from my room and vacuuming the carpets. I've been running the essential oil diffuser, so the aroma of fresh lavender wafts through the space. I also stocked up on Maddie's favourite espresso and picked up fresh flowers at Trader Joe's on my way home.

Despite having just spent hours on a plane, Maddie looks radiant in a red-and-blue boho dress with flutter sleeves and delicate white embroidery. Her hair is pulled back in a high chignon tied with a silk ribbon. She's also wearing colourful blue-and-red eyeglasses. My guess is that she picked up this stunning dress at some Paris flea market, like she always does. Maybe she'll let me borrow it before I leave for Shanghai.

I'm relieved she's back. The last two weeks have been a roller coaster of highs and lows, with a Broadway show, a lawsuit, and a gambling debt thrown in. It's been exhausting. But Maddie's mere presence is already cheering me up.

"So, how was your trip?" I ask, after she's put down her things.

"Amazing. Incredibly productive and so romantic. James booked this gorgeous boutique hotel for us in Saint-Germain. It was really special," she says.

I grin. I'm thrilled for Maddie. She deserves to be happy.

"That sounds amazing. And the fashion school? Did you meet interesting people there?"

"Oh, yes, that was the best part! We had good meetings, and some faculty members took us on a tour of local studios. You would have loved these teachers, Clementine. Many of them are into eco-fashion and sustainability — you know, all the topics you love."

I wish I could have been there. Those are the kind of conversations that make my spirit soar.

"And my parents?" I ask hesitantly. "Did you see them, too?" Maddie's close to my mom, and they always get together when she goes to Paris. I know they talk about me. Despite my mother's diva-esque behaviour and gauche ways, I know she cares.

"Yes, of course. We had lunch. They miss you, Clementine. Your dad is so excited about your going to Shanghai. And so proud! He's told your entire extended family about it. I think it's safe to say you'll be getting a warm welcome."

This makes me think of Henry. That's another warm welcome waiting for me over there. I've considered whether or not to tell Maddie about him and ultimately decided not to; it's just a friendly exchange and I don't want to make a big deal out of it.

"Here, my sweet cousin, I brought you back a little gift." She pulls out a large white box with a red velvet ribbon. First the skirt from Jake and now this! I'm not having such a bad week.

"Oh, Maddie, what did you do?"

"It's actually from your mom. We picked it out together." This makes me smile. I need to stop being so hard on my mom.

I open the box, and my pulse quickens. Inside is a multicoloured cross-body handbag delicately crafted out of strips of velvet and linen.

"It's gorgeous! I love it!"

"I knew you would. It's by a French designer from Toulouse. She only makes a handful of these bags, all stitched together by hand. It's a one of a kind, like you."

I feel all warm inside. It's not always easy being different, especially in the fashion school crowd. Sometimes I think I should try to blend in more, but my quirky ways always draw me back — it's just who I am. And Maddie supports me in my uniqueness. "Thank you so much," I say, slinging the bag across my chest and running over to the hallway mirror. "For everything, Maddie."

"My pleasure. That bag is so you," she says, admiring the effect. "And how was your time without me, young lady? Did you manage okay? Did you eat?" she asks, glancing around with concern. She can tell I haven't used the kitchen much.

"Okay, I guess."

"Okay? Anything happen that I should be aware of?"

I shrug my shoulders. I don't want to talk about negative stuff right now.

She rummages through her suitcase and pulls out a lavender box. "This is the best tea in the world. It's from Mariage Frères. I brought some macarons, too. Let's have some. But — first things first." She grins like a little girl and runs to her room, then comes out a minute later wearing her favourite Minnie Mouse pyjamas.

I can't help but smile. She looks like a teenager.

"I'd love to do the same, but it'll have to wait. I'm meeting Jonathan in an hour."

But seconds later, as if he's somehow picked up on my thoughts, I get a disappointing text from Jonathan.

So sorry, sweetie, I have to push back our date. I need to consult with my lawyer ASAP about my testimony. I'll call you later, okay? Miss you XOXO

And just like that, I go from happy to not.

Maddie senses my disappointment. "Maybe we should have a glass of wine instead. We can have tea in the morning."

I've read Buddhist teachings that warn against attachments. According to Buddhism, we suffer because we get too attached to things or people, and it makes us sad when we lose them or when things don't go according to plan. I think of Buddha as I take a deep breath and try letting go of my expectations about tonight. And then I respond as maturely as I can.

"Yes, a glass of red would be awesome."

I pop a raspberry-flavoured macaron into my mouth and wait for the flavour to explode. Sometimes in a girl's life, macarons fresh off the plane from Paris are the only thing that can save the day.

Chapter Thirteen

"SO, TALK TO ME. What's been going on around here?" Maddie says, curled up on the couch. She's changed her glasses for the tortoiseshell pair she wears at home. She's also wearing socks with lilac unicorns on them. She looks uber comfortable.

I've changed into my zebra-print flannel PJs and covered my legs with a fuzzy pink blanket. While I was changing, Maddie rummaged through the cupboards to find her favourite tortilla chips. She threw them into a bowl and opened a package of guacamole. Now we're snuggled together on opposite ends of the couch.

After my third macaron and a few slugs of decadent red wine, I'm living up to my half-French origins and high on sugar. I just know the crash will be brutal.

I take a deep breath to steady myself before I start talking. "Well, Jonathan's being called to testify against one of his clients in a criminal trial, and Jake's in serious financial trouble. Oh, and I'm going to be leaving for Shanghai in the middle of it all."

"Oh my god," says Maddie. "I'm sorry I haven't been here for you, Clementine. Why didn't you call me? We could have FaceTimed."

"I didn't want to bother you." I take another sip of wine. I'm leaving out the worst details — about sexual assault and loan sharks — for the moment.

"I'm sorry to hear Jonathan is going through that. And Jake, too. But they're both resourceful. They'll get through it." She gives me a reassuring smile. I nod back gratefully.

"And please, don't worry about China, okay? You're putting way too much pressure on yourself. You'll do amazingly well, I just know it. And you're going to have a blast over there! Shanghai is so much fun! I promise you won't even miss New York while you're there." She flashes me a big grin, as if she knows something I don't.

It could be the wine, but part of me believes she's right that I might not even miss New York.

And that might be the real reason I'm feeling so sad.

"So here's my idea," I say to Maddie while she rinses out the chip bowl.

"I'm all ears."

"I'm thinking of asking my dad to represent Jake's skirt collection at his shop. Selling some of his items in Paris would help him out big time."

Maddie stands on tippytoe to put away the dishes. "That's a really sweet thought, Clementine ..."

I purse my lips. "I sense a *but* coming ..."

"Yes, there's a but. Mixing family, friends, and money is never a good idea. What if things turn sour? Do you really want to go down that road?"

"I've told my dad all about Jake's collection before, and he seemed really impressed with Jake's work. He even asked to see samples."

"Of course he's interested. Your dad is forward-thinking, and lots of things about Jake's work are very impressive. But Jake is just starting out, and he hasn't finished his degree yet. He may lack the experience to launch so quickly. You don't want him to crash and burn."

She dims the kitchen lights. To me, it feels as though she's dimming Jake's future. My heart sinks. The last thing I want is for him to crash and burn. Coming face to face with the voice of reason is tough.

She can tell I'm deflated. "I know he's very talented, and I know how much he means to you. I'm just not sure it's a good idea, that's all. And you know how demanding your father can be."

"True." My dad is a perfectionist. Although I doubt there would be serious problems, I guess you never know for sure. But the skirt Jake created for me is spectacular — almost the quality of haute couture.

"Wait till you see the gorgeous silk taffeta skirt he made me. Here, look." I pull out my phone to show her a picture.

"Wow, that really is beautiful," Maddie says, removing her glasses to inspect the photo up close. I suspected the photo might change her mind! "You're a good friend to Jake. I shouldn't rain on your parade. Go for it, if you're sure." She kisses me on the cheek, yawns, and waves good-night as she disappears into her room.

ISABELLE LAFLÈCHE

I start texting Jake immediately, excited to share my plan. I'll take hope and positivity over doubt any day. Right now, any small amount of hope will do.

> Hey are you still up?

Of course. I hardly sleep these days.
What's up buttercup?

> I have a plan …

Ok … not sure I like the sound of that.
Does it involve some kind of questionable scheme? Cuz I'm not sure I could
deal with that — far too much on the line

> No funny business! It's simple actually:
> I think you should create a capsule
> collection of skirts to sell at my dad's
> store in Paris

For a moment, nothing happens in our chat. I imagine the look of surprise on his face, and this puts a huge smile on mine.

WHAAAT? Paris? OMG that would be
a dream! Did your father agree to it???

> Not yet, but I'm sure he will. He loves
> what you do

WOWZA!!!

I switch over to FaceTime. When his face appears, it fills the whole screen. He's grinning and cheering.

"Clementine, you really are the best! How can I ever repay you?"

"How about you start by repaying your debts, once you get some sales? When it's all done, you can buy me dinner at the Russian Tea Room."

"That sounds marvelous," he says in a hoity-toity accent. "Thank you so much, Clemy." I detect a tear of joy in the corner of his eye. Just seeing him this happy improves my outlook on life.

Chapter Fourteen

THEY SAY YOUR outer circumstances reflect your inner ones. Judging by the pile of clothes scattered on my bed, I'd say that couldn't be more accurate. I'm frazzled by the tsunami of news that's hit me over these last few weeks, and Henry's video keeps replaying in the back of my mind. So I'm doing what any fashion student would in an effort to relax: I'm packing outfits for Shanghai.

Everybody's been saying how much fun the city is, with its cool restaurants, clubs, and cafés, so I do need some funky clothes. Thankfully, Jake has come over to help.

He's sitting on my tufted pink chair sipping iced coffee, while old J.Lo songs play on my iPad. It's Saturday morning, and Maddie's at her yoga class. Thank god, because she needs to be totally zenned out when she comes back and sees this gigantic mess.

"I can't forget anything." I'm rifling through my closet looking to see if there are any more clothes I want to bring. My plan is to get everything cleaned and folded neatly before I pack my suitcase. This is unusual for me.

Normally, I would just throw everything into the suitcase and hope that it closes.

"I still can't believe you're leaving next week. I'll miss you, Clemy. Who am I gonna give a hard time to now?"

"Oh, I'm not worried. You'll find a way to get to me. You always do."

He offers a shy smile instead of his typical rambunctious response. He takes off his baseball cap and takes a seat on my bed, crossing his legs to reveal rainbow-striped socks. "How's Jonathan? Is he managing okay?"

I shrug. "I guess, given the circumstances," I say vaguely. "He'll be all right. He's a survivor, like you."

"Right," he says absentmindedly. He starts picking through all the stuff strewn haphazardly on my bed — vintage dresses, cut-off jeans, vintage T-shirts, boho bags, colourful notebooks, coloured gel pens, organic cosmetics, and other trinkets — with an air of concern.

"You're not bringing all of this, are you? It looks like the inside of a recycling bin. You'll need a U-Haul with wings to get all this stuff to China. I think you need to pare down."

I burst out laughing at the thought of Jake suggesting a pared-down life. "Look at the pot calling the kettle black," I say, pointing to his giant man bag overflowing with sketches, fabric swatches, Snickers bars, and various beauty potions.

He cracks a half smile.

"We've been over this already, but I think you need a wardrobe upgrade, girl. You can't be waltzing around the Condé Nast Center looking like a poster girl for the Salvation Army. You need to up your game."

Ouch. That stings. Jake knows I take great pride in my vintage savoir faire, and besides, second-hand thrifting is good for the environment. I remember the Lisa See quote in Henry's video: "Don't ever feel that you have to hide who you are."

"I get what you're saying, but that is my style, you know? *Some* people call it quirky and fun."

"Well, I know, but maybe it's time to embrace something new," Jake replies. "Minimalism is the new in-thing. Less is more."

"That's not exactly the style of those skirts you made. Speaking of which, did you manage to get those samples to my dad yet?"

A pained expression comes across Jake's face.

Uh-oh.

Something's off. Like colossally off. I flash back to Maddie's warning about mixing friends, family, and money. Damn it, I should've listened. Maddie's always right. The last thing I need is for my dad to be pissed off at me. I inhale deeply, trying to stay calm, and kneel on the floor next to Jake.

"What's the matter?" I ask softly.

He looks at the floor and rubs the edge of my bedspread between his fingers.

"You can tell me anything, Jake. Whatever it is, it's okay. You're like a brother to me."

He turns a deep red and finally lifts his face. His eyes are brimming with tears. "Oh, Clemy, I'm such a shit. I was so excited about selling in your dad's store, and I was determined to do things right. But when I cashed the cheque, I thought that maybe I could use it to make some more money, then I'd be able to buy better fabrics and really impress your dad. I wanted to show him the extent of what I can do. I thought one poker game wouldn't hurt — I could always quit if it wasn't working. But I just kept going and ... I lost it. I lost all your dad's money. I'm so sorry, Clem."

"You gambled again? After everything that's happened?" I feel my face growing hot. I know Jake has an addiction he's not in control of, but I can't help feeling upset that he would mess up this chance to help himself, especially after I vouched for him.

Seeing my reaction, Jake bursts into tears. Watching him face his downward spiral again, my anger melts into fear for him, and I begin to cry, too. I realize now just how helpless I am against what's happening to him. What are we going to do? I wrap my arms around him and hold on tight.

"I'm so ashamed," he sobs. "I just couldn't help myself."

I caress his hair. "It'll be all right Jake, we'll figure this out. Just please try not to do this again, okay?" I get up and wrap my fuzzy blanket around his shoulders.

"I'll try my best, Clem," he sniffles. "I'll try."

Despite my best efforts to concentrate in the Parsons library, I can't help but feel storm clouds hovering over my head. I've tried eating gummy bears, drinking bubble tea, and walking Union Square, but nothing's helped.

I'm desperately trying to focus and study for my finals, which is not easy when your bestie is suffering a serious gambling addiction, your boyfriend is agonizing over having to testify against his best client, and your father is about to throw a fit because he paid advance money for skirts that aren't coming.

It just cannot get any worse, I think, twirling my pink polka-dot pen between my fingers.

But it does. The buzz of a text message interrupts my reverie. The woman sitting to my left gives me a dirty look as I pick up my phone.

So who the hell is HENRY LEE?

I drop my phone onto the table like it's given me an electric shock and jump out of my seat. OMG. Jonathan must be pissed — he never uses all caps in his texts. Ever. And he seems uncharacteristically jealous. How did he even find out about Henry? I pick up my phone again, open Instagram, and scroll through my feed. Then it hits me … earlier, I posted a picture of the pile of clothes on my bed with a caption about getting ready for Shanghai, and one of the comments was from Henry: "Can't wait to see you!!!" Jonathan must have gone to Henry's page and seen that I follow him. My stomach ties itself into knots the size of a street pretzel. The woman next to me shakes her head and sighs. Right this second, I wish I could disappear.

Guilt washes over me. Why did I ever correspond with Henry? Am I subconsciously sabotaging my relationship with Jonathan? I'm feeling defensive as well — why is Jonathan stalking my Instagram page like this?

Just as I'm about to respond that Henry is a fellow student and that we're just online friends, the woman next to me interrupts my thoughts.

"Can you please turn off your phone? It's annoying for those of us around here trying to study."

"Sure. Sorry." I shut off the phone and let my head fall to the desk. Maybe that will soothe my pounding headache. I'll respond to Jonathan later.

Dearest J,

Henry is a fashion student at Conde Nast. We're just pen pals. He's been helpful, sending me info about the school. THAT'S IT.

I understand you're under lots of pressure and I know where you're coming from — I had my moment last semester with Stephanie.

But please don't do this to us. Don't create conflict. Not now. You know that my love runs deep.

Clem XO

Chapter Fifteen

"I'M NOT GOING TO CHINA!" I shout into the empty apartment as soon as I set foot in the door. Probably, anyone within a ten-mile radius has just heard me. I just needed to announce it out loud to convince myself that I've decided to stay in New York.

I throw my school bag on the floor and head for the couch. I just want to lie there and stare at the ceiling. I need silence. I crave peace. I want to be alone with my thoughts so I can make sense of what's happening. I know things aren't as simple as I made them out to be in my text to Jonathan. I wish Henry had never written to me.

What I don't expect is to see Maddie walk into the room, with James close behind, a glass of red wine in one hand and a bottle in the other. I turn the colour of his Merlot. I guess the apartment wasn't empty after all. Now I've embarrassed myself. That's all I need.

"What on earth are you talking about, Clementine?" Maddie asks. "Everything is set. The school is waiting for you, your parents are supporting you, and so are we. It'll be the experience of a lifetime. Changing your mind at the last minute would be a huge mistake. What's going on?"

I can't bring myself to look at her. I'm ashamed, embarrassed, and insecure. I don't know what to think anymore, or what to say, so I just stare up at the ceiling, clutching a throw pillow. After I left the library, I tried to figure things out by taking a long walk in the rain. I strolled through the East River State Park in Williamsburg, which has unobstructed views of Midtown Manhattan. I just wish my heart were unobstructed, too.

As I walked, I mentally replayed today's events and those of the last few weeks. Am I just a bystander caught in the middle of a hurricane? If so, why do I feel so guilty about all this drama, as if it's somehow my fault? I finished my walk feeling no clearer than when I'd started and soaked to the bone.

"I can't leave for China, not now. There's just too much going on," I finally tell Maddie. The thunder outside shakes the room a little, as if lending gravitas to my statement.

"There's never really a great time for anything, Clementine," James interjects. "But when opportunity knocks, you have to open the door." Maddie shoots him a look that says *please don't*. She shoos him back to the bedroom, then, once we're alone, shoves my feet over and takes a seat next to me.

"What happened? Is it Jonathan?" She gently removes a strand of hair from my eyes.

I nod, tears running down my cheeks. "Well, sort of. There's more to it."

"What is it, then? Is it about Jake?" She caresses my hair gently, like a caring mother would. A soothing touch, that's what I need. I can't tell her about Jake's gambling addiction, though. She might tell my father, which would make things worse.

"There's … stuff happening to both of them, and they need me here right now."

She smiles kindly at me. "Is it about them, or is it about you? Are you running away from your own potential? It's normal to be afraid, Clementine. Shanghai is far away, and it's okay to feel insecure. I've been there — I felt the same way when I got my scholarship to London. But you need to push beyond your fear. You need to be unafraid to shine. If Jake and Jonathan really love you, they'll support you. And they'll be here waiting when you get back. Besides, your being away will give them the space they need to resolve their own issues. It's nice to feel needed, Clementine, but they'll manage without you."

The voice of reason has spoken. It's like living with a guru. I guess her wisdom comes from life experience, something I don't have much of. The storm outside seems to be subsiding, as if her wise words have calmed not only me, but Mother Nature, too.

I open up about Jonathan, because that's what hurts the most right now.

"Jonathan was acting jealous and possessive today."

Maddie caresses my braid. It's looking messy and out of sorts, thanks to the rain. I guess it matches my mood.

"Really? That doesn't sound like him."

"This guy Henry commented on my Instagram post. He's just a fashion student I connected with online. I think he's stylish, but that's it. There's nothing to be jealous of."

"Unfortunately, that kind of overreaction is part of every relationship," she says. "Is he a Parsons student?"

"No, he's at Condé Nast in Shanghai."

She looks at me and begins to laugh. "Well, of course Jonathan's jealous. You're going off without him! Don't worry, deep down, men love a little competition." She winks.

She's probably right. This is all very silly and there's no need for me to worry.

I stare out the window. What I wouldn't give to see a rainbow. "I guess being involved in a sexual assault case will make a guy overreact," I mutter without thinking.

Maddie's wineglass falls to the floor and shatters, and the little wine that was left in it splashes out. She doesn't even blink, her eyes riveted on me.

"Is everything okay out here?" James bursts out of Maddie's bedroom, where he's been waiting. He sees the broken wineglass on the floor and runs to the kitchen to fetch some paper towels.

"Yeah, it's all good. Just Maddie acting up," I say, trying to keep things light. I don't want anybody to freak out.

"The glass just slipped out of my hands," Maddie says calmly as James mops up the spill at her feet. "Thanks for taking care of that. You're a gem."

James reaches over for a quick kiss.

"All right, then, I'll get back to my cave while you two finish your chat," he says.

As soon as he shuts the bedroom door, Maddie resumes her intense stare. "What on earth is this criminal trial about, Clementine?" she whispers.

"One of Jonathan's clients has been charged with sexual harassment and assault, and Jonathan's going to have to testify as a character witness against him. He has nothing to do with any of it besides knowing about the client's slimy reputation."

Relief spreads across her face, then a frown. "Oh, dear. I can see how that might be stressful."

"He just wishes he didn't have to get involved and he's worried it'll affect his livelihood negatively. But he's got to do the right thing …"

"I hope it works out, for the sake of this guy's victims." She blows out the candle she lit after I got home.

"Now you know why I want to postpone my trip to China," I say softly.

"But this isn't about you, Clementine. You don't need to take this onto your shoulders, or try to solve everybody's problems. Let Jonathan figure things out. You need to take your own responsibilities seriously. You've already committed to going to China. You can't back out now."

"You're right."

I get up from the couch and head to my room to debrief with myself, under the covers with my phone. For the first time in a very long time, I'll need to figure this out on my own.

Rather than let negative thoughts churn needlessly in my mind, I check out my blog traffic. There's been a steady increase in overseas visitors, and I have more readers in China. I guess it was a good idea to open that WeChat account and start cross-posting my blog content and photos there. This puts a smile on my face. Finally some good news.

I wish I could call Jake, just to hear his comforting voice, but I don't want to disturb him.

I jump on to Instagram, hoping to see some cool images and read some inspirational quotes. I see that Henry's online. That makes sense, since it's late morning over there.

He just posted a lovely photo of himself and a friend a minute ago. They're standing in front of tall windows in what looks to be a modern high-rise. He looks happy. It kind of makes me want to be there, away from all the drama here.

> Hey Henry, great shot! Where are you?

He's with a friend, so I don't really expect a response, but I get one right away.

> Clementine, you're still up at this hour?!
> I'm still in Hong Kong, hanging out
> with my pal Stephen before he goes
> back to New York. Are you up doing
> homework?

I have goosebumps. I sit up straight in bed and pull my hair back in a loose ponytail before I continue texting.

> Yeah, finishing up a project. Just taking
> a quick break. What're you guys up to?

> Visiting an amazing fashion exhibit at
> the Museum of Art. It's about costume
> design. You'd love it!

> Sounds awesome. That's
> totally up my alley.

I know! Read your last post on Bonjour
Girl. Good stuff. I showed Stephen your
blog and now he's a fan too. You're
becoming a major influencer ;-)

This last comment gives me the chills. When I first
launched *Bonjour Girl*, my goal was to be read extensively,
but nobody has ever called me an influencer before. Is that
really how he sees me?

Wow, thanks so much for the
compliment:)

Of course! Can't wait to meet you.
Less than a week now, right?

Yup, so much to take care of before
I go. Feeling totally stressed out!

Don't worry, just go with the flow! Gotta
go now, my friend is waiting for me.
Catch you later, okay? Take care and
get some beauty sleep! Not that you
need it ;-)

Oh boy, he's totally flirting. I'm reminded of Jake's
comment about being in trouble — we're going down a
slippery slope. I decide not to respond to that last bit. I end
our exchange with a smiley face emoji.

I follow Henry's advice and go to sleep. You can't think
straight fuelled by pressure and exhaustion, anyway.

Chapter Sixteen

IT'S FINALLY HERE.

The big day. The day I've been both anticipating and dreading. Roses and thorns, champagne bubbles and flat ginger ale, all mixed into one.

Although I'm flying off to Shanghai for an exciting adventure, there's sadness around me. That's probably why I decided to wear black jeans with a grey sweatshirt and black sneakers, something I would never normally wear, for the flight.

Maddie shed a few proud tears this morning after I woke up for our last breakfast together, then we spent the day in New York hanging out. She took me for the best veggie burger, sweet potato fries, and cheesecake in Brooklyn, knowing that I'd miss them in China. Then we hit the Duane Reade and I shopped my heart out for fun toiletries and airplane snacks.

Now I'm sitting in the back seat of an Uber between Jake and Jonathan. It's befitting of how I've felt over the last few weeks — like I'm filling in the holes in their dark places. Now it's time to set myself free. I try to keep a smile on my face between my travel companions' frowns.

I'm looking ahead with confidence. No more wallowing, no more pity parties. While my two favourite men stare out their respective windows, I mentally prepare for the long flight and exciting times ahead. I'm ready to turn the page and have the time of my life.

Jonathan reaches for my hand and squeezes it tightly. Worrying about his upcoming testimony is really draining him.

I squeeze his hand back, and his eyes meet mine. They're filled with tenderness and hope. I blink at him as if to say *don't worry*. It's our own special language. He blinks back. Everything will be all right. I kiss him tenderly.

"Okay, lovebirds, I should have stayed home," Jake says. Like me, he's dressed in black and grey with a black baseball cap. His arms are crossed, and he's been uncharacteristically silent during the entire car trip. His money worries are draining him, too.

"Come on," I say, "you know how much I love you!"

"I just wish …" His voice trails off. "Nah, forget it. I'm just feeling selfish. You totally deserve this. I'm going to miss you like crazy, Bonjour Girl."

"I'm seriously going to miss you, too, Jake." I pat his knee, trying to stay optimistic for both of us, and give him a big peck on the cheek. He smiles and tears run down his cheeks, the droplets hitting his grey pants.

Then the three of us sit in silence, holding hands. The closing scene from *The Breakfast Club* pops into my head, punctuated by that iconic song by Simple Minds: "Don't You (Forget About Me) …"

After my long, sad goodbye with Jake and Jonathan and my mad dash to the gate, I'm finally in the air en route to Shanghai. I've got my laptop out, and I'm about to start working on a new blog post when I feel a tap on my shoulder.

"Clementine? Clementine Liu?"

I look up to see a handsome young Asian man standing in the aisle next to me. He's wearing a stylish jacket and the kind of sneakers that are all the rage these days, plus a cool pair of sunglasses perched atop his head. I feel like a sad creature compared to him. I'm tempted to say that he's got the wrong girl, but instead, the more mature part of me nods.

"Yes, that's me."

"I have a note for you from a close friend of mine." He holds out a folded piece of paper. "Enjoy your flight, okay?"

"Thanks." I reach for the paper clumsily. The man hovers over me, looking right at my laptop screen as though he's trying to read what's on it. I frown and he looks away. Weird.

"Nice to meet you," I say as he heads back to his seat.

The woman sitting next to me gives me a grin. She probably thinks he's my boyfriend or a secret admirer. I smile back, showing some teeth — I don't like to disappoint my audience.

I open the note and my eyes nearly pop out of their sockets. It's from Henry.

Dear Clementine,
I had a feeling you'd be on this flight with
my friend Stephen. Can't wait to finally
meet you! I'm picking Stephen up at the air-
port, so I'll see you soon!
Henry XO

My throat tightens. I feel pounding in my chest. I twirl Jonathan's mother's ring on my finger while I read Henry's note again, feeling a mixture of panic and excitement, guilt and euphoria. What *is* this emotion?

I look down at my boring, sweaty outfit and chastise myself for not bringing a change of clothes in my carry-on. I don't even have my toiletry bag to freshen up before landing. This is the worst.

I take a deep breath and tell myself to stop being so vain. I must have a comb or a brush in my backpack, and I've got some cherry lip balm. That'll have to do.

I sigh loudly and decide that there's only one thing to do, and that's what my best friend would do under these circumstances: I reach for the cupcakes Jake's mother baked me and take a huge bite out of one. I feel better already.

I just hope that feeling lasts.

Chapter Seventeen

THE PILOT'S VOICE comes on overhead, waking me with a start — something about turbulence and needing to put on our seat belts.

The older woman sitting next to me has vanished. She must be in the bathroom. I've actually been enjoying her as a travel neighbour. With her sparkling eyes and warm smile, she's been like a warm security blanket, my only point of reference on this packed plane besides Henry's messenger friend, Stephen, who's sitting two rows over and is far too busy taking selfies to pay attention to me.

I twist and turn in my seat, thinking of Henry. Is he trying to charm me before I even land? He hardly knows me, other than my blog posts and our few text exchanges. He should give a girl some space, and maybe some time to settle in and take a shower. I feel kind of gross now, after sleeping for five hours and eating all those cupcakes. I pull his note from my jeans pocket and reread it. Despite my apprehension, I *am* pretty excited about meeting him in person. If he's as kind in real life as he is in his texts, it won't matter what I'm wearing when we meet.

I reach for my almonds and pop a few into my mouth. Thank god I had the good sense to buy some healthy snacks at the Duane Reade — otherwise, I'd be showing up in Shanghai on a frantic sugar high.

After drafting an article for my blog about the challenges of packing and preparing for a semester of school in China, I open one of my magazines and read about Shanghai Fashion Week, fast becoming one of the most sought-after tickets in the fashion world, along with Labelhood, the event's fashion incubator and one of the most interesting research hubs I've heard about. It's a place that nurtures culture and allows Chinese design talent to experiment.

Then I read up on the city itself: its many karaoke bars, cafés, shops, and markets, as well as the neighbourhood where I'll be staying, the French Concession. A relic of China's colonial past, it's defined by European architecture, cafés, tree-lined streets, manicured gardens, and indie clothing boutiques. Apparently, it's the most atmospheric and captivating quarter of the metropolis. The French Concession was a territory within Shanghai which was ceded to France during the colonial era in 1849 until 1943.

Maddie told me that there are cafés in the neighbourhood where you can get a croissant and a decent *café au lait*. Given my mixed French and Chinese heritage, it sounds like this neighbourhood is going to be perfect for me.

I look up from my guidebook for a second to see my seat neighbour returning.

"That was a long line to use the bathroom," she says in English as I get up to let her back in her window seat. "I'm Sandra, by the way," she says, extending an arm.

"Hi, Sandra, I'm Clementine."

"Oh, what a lovely name."

"Thank you. Are you heading to Shanghai for work?" I ask, sitting up straight in my seat and crossing my legs.

"No, I live there part-time. I'm actually going for family reasons. My sister's not well. I'm going to keep her company and provide mental support while she's in the hospital." She takes a sip of her drink, her gold pinky ring catching the light.

"Oh, I'm sorry to hear that."

"That's kind of you. And what are you doing in Shanghai?" she asks. "Does that adorable young man over there have anything to do with your travels?" She has a mischievous glint in her eyes.

"Him? Oh no, he's just a friend of an acquaintance of mine."

"I see." She looks disappointed. I should try to make the story more exciting for her. My mom is an opera singer, so theatre runs in my blood. Plus, I'd love the opinion of a mature woman.

"Well," I say, twirling my ring again, "it's complicated."

She pats me on the knee and looks at her watch. "We still have nine and a half hours, dear. You can tell me anything. Take all the time you need."

She does look trustworthy, like a family counselor or a therapist. I wonder what she does for a living, but I'm too shy to ask.

I clear my throat. "I have this boyfriend back home. I care for him a lot ..."

"But ..."

"Yes, you're right, there's a *but*. He's been going through some challenges, professionally speaking. This has been hard on him, and it's making him feel a bit insecure." I rub my knee with my hand.

"Challenges can either make or break a relationship."

A flight attendant stops by to offer us drinks. I take advantage of the distraction to inhale deeply and find the courage to continue, once the flight attendant has moved on.

"And then there's this charming student waiting for me at the airport in Shanghai ... His name is Henry. It was his friend who delivered that note earlier. I haven't met him in person yet, but I'm already feeling a growing attraction ... and confusion, if that makes any sense." I feel like I'm blabbering now. I wish Jake were here to calm me down.

"Ah yes, the note. I couldn't help but notice that. Lucky you." She raises her eyebrows, grins, and takes another sip of her drink.

"I don't know if I would call myself lucky. My mind is in a tailspin. I prefer feeling more balanced," I say. That's what I'm craving right now: balance.

"Let me tell you a story," she says, staring deep into my eyes.

I take a sip of Pinot Grigio and tilt my seat back just a little. "Okay, I'm all ears." I need all the guidance and inspiration I can get. Not that there's anything going on with Henry. I'm just happy to get some advice from someone, since Jake is out of reach at the moment.

She looks at me and grins. "You're adorable, Clementine."

"Not always, but I'm glad you think so. Do you have children?" I ask. She shakes her head no. The wine emboldens me to ask, "Did you ever want to?"

"That's a very good question, dear." She stares blankly at the screen before her. "After college, I decided to work in the financial industry. I moved to Hong Kong and began to slowly climb the corporate ladder. There were very few women in finance back then, so I was grateful to find a job and keep it. Then I was promoted to director and, a few years later, managing director. That's a highly coveted position in the industry. I kept at it, trying to play the game. The years passed, and I never had children. The truth is I sacrificed a lot for work, but I'm okay with it. I love my life."

"And now I'm dying to hear your story!" I say in a whisper, moving in closer.

"I grew up in Shanghai. When I was your age, I went off to Yale to study finance. I'd gotten a scholarship, and a cousin of my father's was teaching there. I figured that I would at least know one person at the school, but when I got there, I felt quite disoriented, to be honest. Making friends wasn't easy."

This all sounds familiar. Maybe Sandra and I are soul-mates, just from different generations.

"After a few weeks of attending classes alone, I met a student named Mathias. He had the heart of a poet and a real fire in his belly. He taught me about books, music, and fashion — oh, he loved clothes! We went shopping and dancing and nightclubbing — it was all fun, play, and free-dom. He was a huge fan of the jazz scene, always looking to discover and support up-and-coming musicians. My god, I nearly lost my mind over him! Our chemistry was off the charts. And I fell madly in love. I had never experienced anything like that in my entire life." Her eyes grow wide and her cheeks redden at the thought of her spicy nights with Mathias. I totally get the picture.

"But my father disapproved of our relationship. When I came home for the summer, he intercepted Mathias's love letters and burned them. It was awful."

That sounds devastating. Thankfully, these days, we have the internet and hard drives, but text messages and emails just don't seem as romantic as handwritten letters.

"Because I never responded to his letters, by the time I got back to Yale in the fall, Mathias was in the arms of another woman. And his new flame was so entrancing, that no matter how hard I tried, I couldn't compete."

"Oh, men," I say, trying to sound as though I have years of experience under my belt.

"Years later, when he found out his wife was cheating on him, he contacted me, and we rekindled our friendship. But I never got over the fact that my father ruined my chance to be with the man I loved. The one I should have married. The point of my story is that you don't need to worry. Deep in your heart and in your soul, you will always know who is your true love. You won't even have to guess. It will be obvious. And you'll know what to do."

I lean my head back as a million thoughts rush through my mind. God, I wish I could take Sandra along on my exchange program. I could use her wisdom, what with Maddie and Jake being so far away.

Only time will tell what kind of ending is in store for me. One day, and one time zone, at a time.

I wake up to Sandra tapping me on the shoulder. "You need to put on your seat belt, dear. We're landing soon."

I reluctantly slide my sleep mask up on top of my head and look around as other passengers awaken and straighten their seatbacks.

"I guess that glass of wine knocked me out."

"That's a good thing. You want to look rested when you land, don't you?" She winks.

Once I've come to my senses and gathered my stuff, I turn to see Stephen looking at me. His gaze is so intense, it feels as though he's been staring for a while. It's a bit annoying, but I just wave. He grins and waves back. Unlike me, he looks as fresh as a rose, as though he's just shaved, showered, and changed into a new outfit. In the space of one flight, I've already made two new friends.

In just a short while, I'll be meeting Henry at Shanghai Pudong International Airport. I'm nervous. I've got butter-flies in the pit of my stomach. I recall Sandra's words: "You'll know what to do." This helps me calm down enough that I manage to smile, thinking about the adventures that await me.

Before we land, I scribble my email address, phone number, and blog information on a piece of paper and hand it to Sandra.

"I'd love to keep in touch with you, Sandra. Especially since I'll be far from my family and friends."

A smile spreads across her face. She fishes through her handbag and hands me her business card. "Of course, Clementine. You're like the daughter I wish I had." She pulls out a bag filled with cosmetics and offers it to me. "Here, feel free. You know, before meeting your new friend."

This woman is amazing. I take a peek inside the bag. There's organic rose face spray, lavender hand cream, makeup removing wipes, and some Yves Saint Laurent perfume samples. I smile at her, grateful. I may not be dressed like a Parsons fashion student, but at least I'll smell like one.

"Well, you're like the mother I wish I had," I say, and her face lights up like the sparkling lights along the Bund.

"Thank you for saying that, Clementine."

"I mean it," I reply, just as our captain tells us to prepare for landing.

After spraying some of the refreshing rose mist across my face and soothing my hands with lavender cream, I feel more prepared to hit the ground than I did when we first left New York.

Although we're landing, I feel ready for takeoff.

Chapter Eighteen

"HEY, CLEMENTINE, welcome to Shanghai!"

Oh my. There's no doubt about it: Henry is the definition of handsome. Never mind handsome — he's hot.

I zero in on him, and any travel fatigue I had disappears. I forget that I've just landed in Asia, that I'm sweaty and dishevelled and surrounded by a barrage of different sights and sounds. I'm in one of the busiest airports of the world, but I hardly notice the thousands of travellers rushing around me to find their luggage. I wonder if Sandra would consider this a sign.

Henry greets me with open arms, as though we've known each other for ages. His smile is as devastating in person as it is in his photos, if not more so. He looks as laid-back as can be, without a care in the world.

After Stephen and I have fetched our luggage off the carousel, Henry reaches for my carry-on bag like a true gentleman, and my heart does a few flip-flops.

I can't take my eyes off him.

While we wait for a taxi to take us into the city, I take in Henry's outfit. He's wearing a simple white T-shirt, a blue linen jacket, and classic blue jeans, cool aviator sunglasses, and fine leather shoes. I can tell he's all about understated style and high quality. No cheap fast fashion for this young man. He scores points for that.

His easy smile and friendliness put me at ease so that I don't even feel self-conscious about looking like a rumpled mess. Instead, I feel empowered by the fact that he doesn't seem to care what I'm wearing.

His hair is neatly parted sideways with a bit of gel, reminding me of a young Tony Leung. He was the male lead in my father's favourite movie, *In the Mood for Love*, directed by Wong Kar-Wai. It's set in Hong Kong, and it's about two neighbours who find out their spouses are having an affair and then wonder whether they should do the same. It's about desire and lost love. I guess it reminds my dad of his own challenging love life, and it helps him to see his own life's drama, my mother's infidelities, reflected in a film masterpiece.

"Cool bag, Clementine," Henry says, referring to the funky bag with the sassy slogan that Jake gave me. His English is perfect. He speaks with a hint of an accent, but he's clearly spent a lot of time in the States.

"Thanks. It was a gift from my best friend."

"It suits you!" he says, batting me on the shoulder playfully. I tense up at his touch at first, then immediately melt.

"Thank you so much for picking me up."

"My pleasure. Welcome to Shanghai." He grins and I melt a little more.

I can't believe my luck. But then I remember that I've arrived in a nation whose culture is preoccupied with luck and fortune. I have a feeling that a lot more luck is waiting for me.

"Whoa, Clementine, this place is amazing!" Henry says as we walk into my apartment.

We first dropped Stephen off at his posh high-rise, then Henry came with me to the closest police station to get my fingerprints taken, which is mandatory for all non-residents of China not staying at a hotel. Henry offered to take me out to eat after I've dropped off my bags at the apartment rented by Condé Nast for its exchange students.

"I know! I can hardly believe this place will be mine for the whole summer."

I'm as impressed as he is by the floor-to-ceiling windows and the magnificent view overlooking the courtyard below. Knowing that I'll have this place all to myself makes me giddy. It's a step toward independence: I'll have complete autonomy over what I do, say, and eat, and over the messes I make.

I saunter from room to room like a kid in a toy store, noticing all the details: the touches of pastel, the local art, the many potted plants. There's a small but well-appointed kitchen perfect for making quick meals and hosting my favourite thing in the world, weekend brunches. There's an L-shaped living room with a white sofa and a low coffee table covered with stacks of fashion books. The bedroom is decorated with touches of gold, tiny Buddha statues, and a stack of colourful pillows that give the space femininity and charm.

The main attraction is a large yellow-painted antique desk placed in front of one of the big windows. I can see plane trees, flowers, and people sitting on park benches below. This is where I'll write my blog posts for *Bonjour Girl*. I just know I'll be super prolific and creative here. I can't wait to get started covering local designers and Chinese fashion issues — and to post the piece I wrote on the plane.

Henry flips joyfully through the pages of a large fashion book. His passion reminds me of Jake, and this makes me smile. I guess your vibe attracts your tribe.

"I'm so lucky this place was available. My cousin Maddie says it's really hard to get. I guess it was divine synchronicity."

"You *are* lucky," Henry says with a grin. He seems so at ease with me. Is that a blessing or a curse? "And meeting you is divine synchronicity."

I blush. Here we go again.

"I think you need a painting on that wall over there," Henry says, touching his index finger to his nose thoughtfully, like a gallery owner.

"It is a bit bland, isn't it?" I say, laughing at the all-white walls, something Jonathan would appreciate. I prefer bright pops of colour.

"Yes, the complete opposite of you," Henry says. He's flirting, but it's harmless fun, I tell myself. There's nothing to worry about. Right?

"Oh, stop it. How do you know that? I may just disappoint you by being supremely boring."

"Pfft. I don't buy it!" he shoots back. "But what I am buying is dinner. You must be starving."

"Totally!" I'm also jet-lagged, in desperate need of a shower, and dying to call Jonathan, Maddie, and Jake.

"How about we try a café nearby so I can freshen up first? I'll meet you in an hour."

"Sure. Let's meet at Baker & Spice down the road. They make the best soups. And I'll get you a special coffee to help with the jet lag. Take all the time you need." He disappears into the hallway, leaving a trace of his elegant scent: a mix of lemongrass and neroli. I try not to get too affected by it, but it's tough.

Before contacting anyone, I fall back onto the bed and stare up at the ceiling, just taking a few minutes to soak up this glorious moment.

I've made it halfway across the planet, and I'm about to begin an exciting fashion program. The bullying I faced last semester was just a test to build my inner strength. It was all worth it.

Eventually, I reach for my phone. It's six in the evening here, which means it's six in the morning in New York. I'll take a chance and call Jonathan to wake him with a kiss.

I dial his number, but it goes directly to voicemail. I feel a pang of worry. I hope everything's okay. Then I try Jake and again, get no answer. I finally try Maddie, who picks up with a squeal.

"Hel-lo, Clementine! How was your flight?"

"Great! I slept really well and I met an amazing lady named Sandra. She'll be your temporary replacement," I say.

"Sounds good, as long as it's only temporary! How's the apartment?"

"A dream! It's gorgeous, Maddie. I'm so happy and grateful. I can't thank you enough."

"Now I'm worried that you'll never come back!"

"Very unlikely. I can't stay away from my tribe for too long. How are you doing?

"This place is deathly quiet now. I already miss you."

"Me, too. I wish you were here so we could stroll around the designer studios. I know how fond you are of Chinese fashion."

"I wish I were there, too. There's a amazing store you need to check out called Song Liung. They're committed to promoting up-and-coming local designers. And sustainable fashion, too. Shanghai is on the cutting edge of eco-fashion."

"Yeah, I read about that on the flight." Eco-conscious fashion designers here are leading the way to a greener future with recycled and organic couture. Apparently, in Shanghai, it's easy to find chemical-free baby clothes, bamboo evening gowns softer than silk, and purses made from recycled billboard paper.

"You're going to adore that store. Maybe something to write about on your blog?"

"Sure." This reminds me of Brian's advice. He thought I should write about local stores, designers, and retail. If Maddie likes it, then so do I.

"Okay, I gotta run. I have a dinner date and a call to make before I go," I say, looking at the time. "Can you please let my parents know that I made it here safely?"

"A dinner date already? You don't waste any time, do you? It doesn't sound like you're missing me or anybody!" she teases. This makes me think of something I once read about Shanghai: "New York may be the city that never sleeps, but Shanghai doesn't even sit down."

I have a feeling my life is about to get busy — and that's the way I like it.

"I'm so proud of you for doing this, Clementine," she says. "I know there was some hesitation, but I know you'll come back a changed woman. I'll let you get to your dinner, and don't worry, I'll contact your mom. Have fun, okay?"

After Maddie hangs up, I wonder just how much change I'll be going through.

One more call to make.

"Hey, Ellie. I'm so glad I managed to catch you online," I say, as her face comes into view on FaceTime. "I need to talk to you about something." For the last month, Ellie's been on a short-term exchange program at a Parisian design school that specializes in intricate beading, but she's finally back in New York. She's one strong female friend I can count on.

"How's Shanghai?"

"I just landed, but so far so good. I've already made some friends and I'm looking forward to classes."

"So what's going on?" Ellie asks, taking a sip out of a mug. She looks pretty in a lilac tunic with delicate dragon-fly embroidery on the collar. It contrasts nicely with the tattoo of Marie Antoinette on her arm.

"I can't talk too long right now because someone's waiting for me, but I wanted to tell you that I'm worried about Jake," I begin. Ellie cares about him as much as I do.

"Why? What happened? We FaceTimed a few times when I was in Paris and he seemed okay. Just a bit tired."

"That's what I thought at first, but it's more compli-cated than that. He's all over the place and it's affecting his creativity and his health. He's really struggling to keep up."

She gives me a puzzled look. "Aren't we all?"

She has a point. Balancing school, work, and personal projects requires a gargantuan amount of energy and focus.

And the need to focus on time-intensive activities, such as sewing and drafting patterns and chasing down internships, adds to the pressure of fashion school. Furthermore, studying in New York has a particular downside. It requires money — lots and lots of it. Students who don't come from a wealthy background struggle to make ends meet.

"Yeah, but he's also in serious debt … from gambling. He started off playing online poker, trying to make a little extra cash, and it got out of hand. He's got a full-blown gambling problem." Jake would kill me for talking about this, but I need to know someone's looking out for him while I'm away.

"What?" Ellie's eyes nearly pop from their sockets.

"What's more, he's borrowed from some shady people, and he owes so much that they're threatening his family now."

"Oh my god!" Her purple manicured fingers pop against her skin as she clutches her face.

"Our sweet Jake is in a really bad place."

She looks worried, and I know what she's thinking.

"I don't think Jake would do anything to harm himself," I say, "but we still need to watch for it. I convinced my dad to carry some of Jake's skirts in his shop in Paris, but then Jake gambled the advance money away and failed to deliver his samples. He's so devastated and ashamed about it. I just don't know what to do now that I'm out here. I need your help. We need your help."

She leans forward. "Okay, I'll do it."

"Wait … you'll do what?"

"I'll make sure the skirts are made," she says matter-of-factly.

"Really? Do you have time for that?"

"Sure, I'm not taking any courses this summer. I have a part-time job and that's it. I'll make the time."

"Wow, Ellie, that's great." I'm amazed by her generosity. "But I'm still worried about Jake's safety, with those loan sharks after him."

"I'm not too worried about them," she says, tapping her long nails on her desk.

"No?"

"My brother's in the NYPD. I'll call him if they try anything." She grins.

"Perfect! Thanks, Ellie."

"That's what friends are for, right? We'll figure it out. Jake's been a great friend. It's the least I can do."

I sign off, relieved and filled with hope. I can relax a bit. This will be a good summer after all.

Chapter Nineteen

I ARRIVE OUT OF BREATH at the café Henry picked. It looks and feels like one of those cool New York City coffee shops I love, but with an Asian twist. The menus are written in English, French, and Mandarin, and there's soft lounge music playing. Thankfully, I can read and speak all three languages fairly well, thanks to my dad, who "highly encouraged" me to take Mandarin and English classes all through high school.

On display, there are buttery croissants, soups and sandwiches, and salads. The young women behind the counter are both stylish and friendly, welcoming me with warm smiles. I have a feeling this place will be my favourite hangout.

I'm feeling refreshed in my pink prairie skirt, T-shirt, Adidas sneakers, and layered vintage necklaces, including one that belonged to my paternal grandmother from Beijing and one that belonged to my maternal great-grandmother, Cécile. It's a look that represents the different facets of my heritage.

Henry waves at me from a tiny corner table, looking relaxed and perfectly at home.

"Hi there." I take a seat. There's a cappuccino waiting for me with a heart drawn in the foam. That video, and now this heart. Is this a subtle message?

I decide not to make anything of it. Henry has a leaf drawn in his foam. Maybe it's just luck of the draw.

"Do you mind?" I ask, taking out my phone. I want to take a picture of our coffees and post it on my blog to announce that I've landed safely in Shanghai. I know Jake and Ellie will both get a kick out of it.

"Of course not. I just did the same myself," he laughs. "I ordered some soup for us, I hope that's okay. This isn't the most traditional cuisine, I know, but I'll make it up to you some other time, I promise. I know a few excellent traditional restaurants that will blow your mind."

I refrain from mentioning the restaurant Jake mentioned, but I smile to myself, thinking about its silly name and the plastic hair rollers on its walls.

"That would be great," I say, still focusing the phone camera on the foam pictures in our coffees.

"You'll have to add this to your WeChat, too. I saw that you've been posting on there for a while. Your writing style is solid and the social issues you talk about are so important. You'll have a massive following in China in no time."

"Thanks. I'm working on it."

"So how long have you been at it — blogging?"

"Not that long. I used to post more often, but I've been really busy with finals lately. I'm looking forward to posting more frequently again."

He nods, as though taking in what I've said and analyzing every word. I wonder what he'd think of all the advice I've been getting to take a more commercial direction.

"One of my Parsons teachers thinks I should try to monetize my blog. To be honest, I'm not really inclined to go in that direction. But I don't want to disappoint him, either. I'm torn."

He gives me a thoughtful look. "It's always important to stay open to new ideas and concepts. It's the only way to grow as an artist."

That was not what I was hoping to hear. Oh well. *Just let it go, Clementine.*

Henry points to my cup. "You'd better drink your coffee before it gets cold."

"Oh, right." I lift my cup and take a long comforting sip. At the first jolt of caffeine, I feel like myself again.

"Thanks for this. It's just what I needed."

"My pleasure. I'm used to that flight route. I know how exhausting it can be."

"So what did you study in New York? Was it fashion related?" I take another sip. The caffeine is really kicking in now.

"I studied environmental sustainability at NYU. That's why I sit on a panel at school about eco-fashion. It's my expertise from undergrad." His eyes twinkle. I can tell he loves what he does — that's part of what makes him so magnetic.

One of the young baristas shows up with our soup. I dig right in.

"So, Clementine, tell me more about why you decided to come to Shanghai."

"Upward mobility," I joke.

"You don't strike me as someone who cares about stuff like that."

"You're right, I don't really. But you know how New Yorkers can be obsessed with financial success. I'm just here to learn and have fun, expand my knowledge and my horizons. The timing wasn't great, but I'm happy to be here now."

"Nothing negative, I hope?"

"Just some personal stuff that was tough to leave behind."

"Do you mean Jonathan?" he asks matter-of-factly.

"Whoa. You've really done some deep research, haven't you?" I say, blushing. Why did I never mention Jonathan to him in our texts?

"Yep, you can find out pretty much anything on social media these days. I came across a picture of you two at a Parsons gala last fall."

"Yes, he's a really special guy."

Henry's gaze is intense, and so is my inner reaction to it. This is uncomfortable. Waves of guilt and unease wash over me. I'm not sure what more to say, so I take another sip of coffee. He changes the subject.

"I'm heading a panel next week about the effect of blue jeans manufacturing on rivers. I put down your name as a guest. I hope you'll be there."

"That sounds terrific, of course I'll be there. It could make a great topic for a blog post."

He gives me a curious look — I'm not sure why. This time, I change the subject.

"Maddie suggested that I visit the Song Liung boutique. I assume you know it?"

"Oh yeah, it's a great place. We could meet there tomorrow if you'd like, before your classes start."

"Cool, I'd love to see some of the fashion scene before the semester begins. I've heard so many great things about the local designers. And I'm excited about classes, too ..."

"I think you're going to love the program. It goes into a lot of depth, and the teachers are on point." He wipes his fingers with a napkin. "And I think the school will benefit from having someone with your vision in it."

"Right back at you."

"If you need anything, anything at all, just WeChat me, okay?" he says.

"Sounds good." We get up from our chairs, and I hesitate a moment before giving him a friendly hug to thank him for all that he's done for me today. He gives me a look that make me feel like he can see right through me. It sends shivers through my body, all the way down to my sneakers. At a loss for words, I blurt out, "Thanks again for everything!" and rush out of the café as fast as I can.

I'm running away from my emotions, my strong attraction to him, and, most likely, from myself.

After changing into track pants and my favourite sweatshirt, I try calling Jonathan again, but again I go straight to voicemail. That's strange. Is there an issue with the trial? I can't help but wonder if I should be worried. I decide to reach out to Jake — that'll make me feel better.

"Hey, you! So happy to see your face! I miss it already!" I say as soon as we connect on FaceTime.

"I miss you, too, pumpkin. How was the flight?"

"Fantastic! I met a fabulous woman named Sandra, and she had the coolest glasses, just like you."

"Oh, fab. I knew you were going to replace me sooner or later. I was hoping it would be later."

"Ha ha. You're number one, remember?"

"Happy to hear. What's that you're eating?" He's referring to the dessert I picked up on my way home.

"It's roasted grass jelly. It's made with an herb called mesona and served with coconut milk. Apparently it's good for digestion." I playfully take a bite in front of the camera. "Mmm, delicious."

"Well, I wish you could FedEx some to me *tout de suite*."

"I would if I could. You'd love the food scene here, especially the street food. They sell all sorts of delicacies across town."

"Ooh, like what?" I can almost hear his mouth watering.

"One thing I can't wait to try is *jianbing*. It's a popular breakfast food. It's kind of like a fried crepe. They spread eggs over the surface of the pancake as it cooks, then they add crunchy strips of fried wonton, cilantro, scallions, and pickles, with sweet hoisin and chili sauce. And each one is cooked to order on a cast-iron grill."

"That sounds amazing! You're making me hungry. Can you please send me pictures when you try it? I'd love that. I can discover the local food along with you."

"Sure, that would be fun."

"So talk to me about that cool café. Who did you go with? Henry?" He grins.

"Uh-huh."

"And?"

"He really *is* attractive and magnetic. Smart, too. It may become a problem."

"I knew it."

"I just need to focus on school, not on men."

"Are you kidding me?"

"That was *your* advice, Jake!"

"Well … happy to hear my wisdom is sinking in."

"I'm working on it, anyway. So what's new in NYC?"

"Ellie's been keeping me super busy today. She's helped me put the finishing touches on the samples and she has me on the night shift, sewing up a storm. They're so beautiful, Clem — you will just die!"

"Let me see!"

He turns his phone to show me the pictures on his computer. They're stunning. I'm not surprised; he and Ellie are super talented.

"They look incredible."

"I'm really grateful. To her and to you." He turns the phone back around to show his face, and points into the screen at me. "I know what you did."

"What did I do?"

"You asked her to take care of me, didn't you?"

"I have no clue what you're talking about." I spoon another bite of dessert.

"Oh, come on!"

"All right. Maybe just a little coaxing on my part."

"Well, your plan is totally working. She's keeping me out of trouble. Off the gambling sites and off the poker tables. You're a genius."

I hold back tears. I miss him so much. And the fact that I could help him out, even in the smallest way, means the world to me.

"I just want you to be happy, healthy, and productive." I point my spoon at the screen, punctuating each word.

"Thanks, Clem. Sending some big love your way." He air-kisses the camera.

I air-kiss him back. "I gotta go finish this dessert now, I'll talk to you later!"

"Enjoy it, babe, you deserve it! Stick to the sweet desserts instead of the sticky men. Mwah!"

Chapter Twenty

I RING THE BELL of the house on Fumin Road and get ready to discover the work of the young designers featured at Song Liung, the trendy boutique Maddie recommended. Needless to say, I'm pretty excited. I'm proud of myself — I took the subway here. Not that subways themselves are a big deal; in Paris and New York, taking the subway is a way of life. But I still think I deserve a pat on the back for navigating alone through this mega metropolis.

I hardly slept last night, thanks to jet lag and to worrying about Jonathan.

I tried calling him a third time, late last night, but his phone was off.

He *did* send me a cryptic text this morning saying he got my message, he's glad the trip went well, and he'll call me later. *Whatever*. I'm going to try not to let this get to me or ruin my day. Following the advice of Cécile's etiquette book once again, I won't overreact, and I will chill out. Maybe the book doesn't word it exactly like that, but that's my interpretation.

I did a bit of research about this store in advance of meeting Henry. It carries clothing lines by twenty young designers from Beijing and Shanghai, including the delicate tailoring of Liu Min and the environmentally friendly designs of Sara Yun. Also, I can't wait to check out the retro sunglasses from CHairEYES that were inspired by old movies.

I like to think of myself as an eco-warrior with a decisive spirit: I choose to buy most of my clothes from thrift shops, consignment boutiques, and flea markets. Most of the time, I enjoy and prefer buying second-hand.

Give me funky, quirky, and original over expensive any day. Not that I don't appreciate high-quality fabrics or clothes — quite the contrary. And a shop that supports local designers and ecological, sustainable fashion makes me swoon.

"Hey, Clementine!" Henry calls out from the shop entrance. He's wearing a plain T-shirt, black jeans, colourful sneakers, and cool aviators. He looks good.

I'm wearing a cream-coloured linen skirt made by a fellow Parsons student, a silk top with embroidered roses, and platform shoes in rainbow colours. I'm also wearing a bright-pink lipstick and funky vintage sunglasses, and I've got my hair down. This look represents how I feel about being here: totally carefree. It also reminds me of something I once read about artist Frida Kahlo: she believed that clothing and fashion connect us to our inner selves and to the world around us. Looking around this amazing store I've just entered, I feel connected, indeed.

"I've asked a friend who works here to show us around," Henry announces.

"Cool."

A young man saunters toward us with a grin.

"Hi, Clementine, I'm Mark. Welcome to Shanghai! Henry told me about you and your blog." He speaks quite good English. "Let me show you around."

I look around the elegant space. It's three floors of contemporary art and jewellery and carefully curated objects. In many ways, it reminds me of my dad's store in Paris.

The majority of the world's clothes, whether for the luxury or the mass market, are manufactured here in China, and a nation of avid fashion consumers has sprung up.

"I think you'll like the work of Liu Min," Mark says, pointing to a display.

"So do I. I've seen her work online. It's beautiful."

"Yes, it's absolutely gorgeous," Henry chimes in. It's refreshing to be surrounded by men who appreciate this kind of beauty.

I take a look at the display of pieces. A blouse that combines a cherry blossom pattern with a more masculine cut catches my eye. It's totally drool-worthy.

Henry sees me admiring it.

"Try it on!"

"Oh, thanks but no thanks. I'm trying to watch my spending."

"It'll be my treat. Your welcome gift to Shanghai. You'll be giving me some coverage of my panel session on your blog. Let this be an informal way of paying you back."

"Well, um, I haven't agreed to anything just yet," I say, putting my hands on my hips playfully. "And I'm just happy to help out — really."

His expression changes subtly; I can tell he's disappointed.

I don't want to offend him, so I politely reach for the blouse and disappear into the change room. I need to work on letting myself be more open to receive. Apparently, in some cultures, saying no to a gift can be a block to friendship.

Moments later, after chatting and taking a selfie with a kind young woman trying on a jaw-dropping dress, I reappear with a huge grin on my face. The blouse does look good with my skirt. I prance around the shop. Mark gives me a thumbs-up, and Henry snaps a photo on his phone.

"Okay, it's a done deal," he says.

I hesitate for a moment. Something about his comment makes this feel transactional, as though he's expecting things from me in return. It makes me feel a bit uncomfortable. Clearly, Henry comes from a wealthy family, but that doesn't make it okay for him to try to buy my friendship or respect. I just don't operate that way.

"Thanks, Henry. But I just can't accept it. It's very generous of you to offer, though."

"It's too late, the blouse is all yours!" He looks over at Mark and grins.

"Really?" I guess he paid for it while I was in the change room. "Then thank you. It's gorgeous."

"The pleasure is all mine," he says.

I nod back, hoping I look grateful. This generous gesture has caught me off guard.

"Next stop, Annata Vintage. You'll love this shop. It's totally you."

"Are you for real? That sounds right up my alley." I can't believe my luck. A man who loves vintage. And then it hits me suddenly that Jonathan has never once accompanied me on any of my thrifting or flea market expeditions, and the thought makes me a little sad.

I just hope to hear back from Jonathan soon, before any feelings for Henry take root.

In the taxi on the way to the vintage shop, I take a second to look at my phone. There's a missed call from Jonathan. My heart tightens, and I feel guilty for missing it, especially while out shopping with another man. I regret accepting the blouse, too, especially when some of the people closest to my heart are struggling financially.

I consider asking the driver to turn around so I can go home and return the call, but Henry changes my mind.

"You're going to adore this place, Clementine. The owners, Julia and Ting, are into recycling and vintage and they have amazing taste."

"Oh yeah?"

"They have racks filled with fantastic vintage pieces. They regularly travel the world to find treasures that capture the look and feel of a 30s Shanghai boudoir. The store's decorated with wallpaper from the 30s and 40s, and it has a little courtyard where they host book exchanges, clothing swaps, and theatre performances."

Wow. He's really piqued my interest. The owners sound so original and creative. I can't turn back now. I'll call Jonathan as soon as I get home.

"That sounds terrific. I'll need to go home after this, though."

"Sure, no problem," Henry responds with a smile. I can tell he likes showing me around this city. And I have to say, he's been totally on target so far.

We arrive in a small alleyway, and as we exit the car in front of a jewel box–sized shop, I hear giggles and the sound of 70s R&B. I'm already smitten.

Henry opens the door, and I walk in, feeling like a child entering a fairyland. I gasp with delight as I take in the small, charming space. It reminds me of some of the cool vintage shops in New York's East Village. The walls are a cool-blue hue, and there's an antique iron bed right in the middle of the store. The owners welcome us with beaming smiles as soon as we walk in.

"Hello, Clementine, I'm Julia," one of them says in accented but perfectly clear English. She's wearing large red glasses, turquoise vintage pants, and a crop top made of pink, purple, and blue silk. She looks supremely cool. "Meet my partner, Ting."

"I'm so happy to meet you both. And I love your store!"

"Thank you! We love your style! We saw the pictures you posted on WeChat," Ting shoots back. She speaks English fairly well, too.

"Oh, thanks." I'm enjoying the compliment, but also confused. "What photos?"

"She's talking about the photos of you in that Liu Min blouse that I shared on WeChat," Henry says.

I guess they were checking out his profile in anticipation of our appointment at their store. The fact that Henry shared photos of me on his account without telling me makes me squirm a little. Normally, I wouldn't want anyone to take pictures of me shopping — that's not something I'd like to share publicly — but in this case, since it involves a shop Maddie recommended and a fashionable local designer, I let it slide.

And the feedback about my style is a really nice boost to my morale. Maybe the universe put the exchange program and Henry in my way so that I could get a move on with my projects on an international scale.

I explore the store some more. My heart races as I admire an orange-and-yellow jacket with dainty butterflies. The label says it's from Japan. The detailing is impeccable. That's why I love vintage so much: unlike some of the shoddy construction you find in fast fashion, the quality in vintage can't be beat. And it's a good viable alternative to fast fashion for people on a budget. I make a mental note to blog about the subject. I find a long cocktail dress with pink and green flowers and an open back that comes together in a large bow. Perfect for an outdoor wedding or a fancy cocktail party. I know Jake would get a total kick out of it.

"Can I take a photo of the back of this dress?" I ask. "For a designer friend back home."

"Sure!" Ting responds.

"You guys have terrific taste," I gush. "I love all the details in the store." Julia and Ting have included handwritten details about the origin of each item on its price tag, such as *70s Japan* or *50s–60s England* — a really nice touch. I take a few pictures for Jake.

After I've inspected every single piece, taken a few pictures for my blog, and tried on a few things, Julia invites me to sit outside, in the courtyard. I select a vintage bistro chair. Ting brings out cups of freshly brewed coffee — a girl after my own heart.

"What great hospitality!"

"People come into the shop from all around the world," Julia says. "We love it when they stay to chat."

"I bet they always do. There's a really nice vibe about the place."

Ting puts on an old jazz record on a portable turntable, and we all sit together under the plane trees and talk about our favourite New York vintage shops, alternating between English and Mandarin. I'm grateful for practice. I take notes on my phone about their favourite places in the city, including cafés, drugstores, and bars.

"Where are you heading next?" Julia asks.

I turn to Henry. I'm about to respond but he answers first. "School. Clementine needs to pick up her school materials."

Oh, right. Henry's brought me back to reality.

"And then home. I have some calls to make."

"What are you studying?" Julia asks.

"Fashion journalism and online media."

"Oh, wonderful."

"Yeah, it's exciting. And it'll help me with my writing. I plan to write about you two, I promise. As soon as I set foot in here, it was love at first sight."

And then I feel Henry's strong gaze on me and I blush, embarrassed that I've uttered those words. I shouldn't have. I don't want there to be any confusion in Henry's mind. Even if there might be some in mine.

Chapter Twenty-One

"JULIA AND TING are so cool! Thanks for taking me to their shop. That was awesome. They're going to be key members of my local tribe."

"I think so, too. I could tell they really liked you."

"Shanghai and I are getting along famously," I say confidently, a huge grin on my face. There's a reason this city is called the Paris of the East.

It's a bright, sunny day that matches my mood. I stare through the window of the taxi as we drive to school, and my senses go into overdrive, taking in the sight of the modern skyscrapers, the people, more skyscrapers and more people. It's like Manhattan on steroids.

We drive through the financial district, one of the most happening neighbourhoods, where many of the city's attractions and landmarks are. Henry points out the Oriental Pearl Tower, the Cruise Port, the History Museum, the Jin Mao Tower, the Natural Wild Insect Kingdom, and the Ocean Aquarium.

"An insect kingdom? No thanks!"

"Oh, come on, insects are some of the oldest animals on earth. How could you not be interested?"

"I just prefer not to get too close to them, that's all."

"Don't you like butterflies? Didn't I see a butterfly print on one of your skirts at your place yesterday? A Japanese butterfly expert once sent thirty boxes of rare butterfly specimens to this museum."

"Okay, I do love butterflies. They're one of my favourite creatures. Not just for their beauty, but also because of the incredible transformation they undergo. I think they're a great metaphor for life."

"Shedding the old skin to become what you're truly meant to be?"

"Yes! And I love seeing them fly, especially the rare kinds. They're mesmerizing."

"Just like you."

My heartbeat accelerates and my face turns a dark shade of pink. "Yeah, I'm just like an insect. The pesky kind!" I say awkwardly. I'm not accustomed to this kind of flirting.

Henry just laughs and looks out the car window. It's pretty obvious he knows what kind of effect he has on me, and he's just lapping it up. "I'll take you there. You'll love it."

I say nothing and just blush some more. What else is new?

A song comes on the radio. The lyrics are about driving in the sun, sharing a special moment with someone you care deeply about. It's a very romantic song. I catch Henry peeking at me out of the corner of his eye. I wonder if he's picking up on the lyrics, too.

Fifteen minutes later, we reach our destination.

"We're here!" Henry announces, pulling out his phone to pay the driver.

"No, it's my turn," I say. "This is school related, and I have an allowance for it."

"If you insist …"

Henry is just really relaxed about money. He has a quiet, refined elegance, too, like the members of old-money families I've crossed paths with on Manhattan's Upper East Side.

We enter the modern Condé Nast building and my heart nearly stops. For real. The facility is truly impressive. I get the same gigantic rush of adrenalin I felt when I first walked into the main Parsons building in New York. It's difficult to explain, but it borders on euphoria. One thing I know for sure is that I've picked the right thing to do with my life. There's no doubt about *that*.

Henry walks me to a large, airy room with colourful floor cushions, low sofas, and bright windows and skylights. It feels like a cool lounge, minus the noise and the drinking. It's actually quite serene, and it makes me feel introspective and reflective.

"This is where all the guest lectures take place. Guest speakers come and lecture here all the time. As a matter of fact, there's a lecture in about twenty minutes by the editor of *GQ Asia*. You wanna listen in on it?"

"I'd love to."

He just grins. It's as if he planned the timing of our visit so that I could hear this talk.

"Okay, we'll come back after you get registered." Henry points toward the admin offices.

"So, what do you plan on doing after graduating?" I ask as we stroll down the hall. A few fashionable students walk by us and nod. Some are dressed in super trendy outfits, but most look relaxed in simple, non-flashy clothing, like jeans and T-shirts. I appreciate this low-key vibe. Just like at Parsons, my quirky style may stick out here, but that's okay.

"I've been thinking a lot about that lately. Maybe I'll launch an eco-fashion NGO, or start my own conscious fashion advertising agency. Or both." He laughs. "Work-wise, I can be pretty intense."

Work-wise? I want to say that his intensity goes far beyond his work life, but I keep that to myself. I don't know him well enough yet. "Those sound like great ideas."

"That's all they are right now, just ideas. But I'm seriously looking into them. What are your plans? Do you want to stay in America? Reach for the stars in the Big Apple?"

"Maybe. I'm not sure yet. I know I want to continue writing. That's part of the plan. And expanding *Bonjour Girl*. Who knows where that will take me?"

"Far. You already have an impressive following for such a short time frame. Have you ever thought of launching your own line of accessories? Or a print magazine for everyday cool girls around the world, one that would appeal to girls of different cultures and backgrounds? I mean, that's your blog's purpose, isn't it?"

I stop in my tracks. Such great ideas. My very own magazine and accessories line? I could even ask Jake and Ellie to help design them. In my mind, a resounding yes pops up in bright, bold technicolour.

"Wow. You just planted a seed. You're a creative genius! You *should* open an agency. I'll be your first client."

He puts his hands in his pockets, gazes at me, and smiles peacefully, as he's done several times since we've met. Quiet assurance — he just knows that he's got it.

At the admin offices, Henry introduces me to the director of the program. Her hair is cut short and she's wearing a long flowing, purple-and-black tunic like the ones Ellie likes to wear, and some cool white-and-black platform shoes.

"Clementine, welcome!" she says in English. "Maddie told me all about you. We're so glad that you'll be spending a semester with us."

"Thanks! Me, too."

"You'll be a great addition to the student body. Here's your welcome package. Read through it, and come back and see me this week if you have any questions, all right?" She smiles, her eyes twinkling kindly. "And we'll see you in class on Monday."

I'm floating on a pink cloud as Henry walks me back to the lounge.

I float even higher when I see the GQ editor looking snazzy in a sharp black suit.

And I nearly go into orbit when Henry, who sits on the school's event committee, introduces me to the GQ editor as an "upcoming blogging sensation."

But the vibration of my phone starts to bring me back down to earth. I see that I have several texts and missed calls. All from Jonathan. How could I have missed these?

When I see texts full of all caps and exclamation marks, I come crashing down faster than a hot air balloon that's run out of propane.

"I'm really sorry," I say to Henry and the GQ editor, "but something's come up back in New York. I need to get home and make an urgent call."

"What? Right now? But what about the lecture?" Henry looks dumbfounded, as does the GQ editor.

"I know, I did really want to hear it. Could you record it for me on your phone? I'd be super grateful."

"Sure," Henry says, sounding deflated. I guess I was right. He did bring me here to listen to the lecture. It *was* planned all along. I feel even worse now.

"I'm really sorry, Henry, I'll connect with you later, okay?"

"I hope it's nothing too serious." I can tell he's trying to discreetly find out more. He can probably pick up on my vibes. I'm sure I'm radiating negativity.

"It'll be fine," I lie.

As soon as the taxi pulls up in front of my building, I thank the driver and rush up to the apartment. I drop my handbag, my keys, and the package containing the blouse on the counter. I grab my phone, and for the first time since I arrived, I sit down at the desk and stare out the windows overlooking the courtyard. This soothes my anxious spirit and nerves enough that I can make the call.

"Hey." Jonathan's tone is curt and dry. I can tell he's angry.

"Hi, is everything okay? You sound upset."

"Well, you tell me, Clementine. I mean, how do you think I feel, knowing that the first thing my girlfriend did after flying halfway across the planet was to go on a coffee date with some guy she met online?"

Oh god. He saw the coffee photos Henry posted. Has Jonathan actually been stalking Henry's WeChat feed?

"And then the cherry on top — or should I say the cherry blossom on the blouse — is you going out shopping with this guy today, while I sit here waiting to lose half my business. If you really are just 'pen pals,' how did you get to be so chummy so quickly, is what I'd like to know!"

I'm frozen, caught in ugly flashbacks of my parents' fights. So much pain and anger.

He sighs loudly. "Look, is there something going on between you two? If there is, just come out and say it, okay? Be honest with me."

Come on, Clem, say something. But I just sit there, tongue-tied, filled with guilt. I understand his frustration, but also hate his possessiveness and petty jealousy. That indignation keeps me from responding.

He sighs again. "Well, since you're not talking … I guess I have my answer. Enjoy Shanghai."

He disconnects.

Horrified and unable to think straight, I run into the bedroom and throw myself onto the bed. I feel terrible and alone. Terribly alone.

How do I get myself out of this bloody mess?

Chapter Twenty-Two

I WAKE UP IN the middle of the night feeling groggy, wondering where the hell I am.

One of my hands is grasping my Minnie Mouse doll, and the other is nestled beneath my pillow. I have no idea what time it is. I slowly drag my way out of sleep.

And then I remember. A wave of guilt washes over me.

And then sadness. I begin to weep.

I feel terrible about what's happened. I probably could have avoided this whole mess. What was I trying to prove with this friendship with Henry, anyway? Was I craving attention because Jonathan wasn't around to provide it?

I *am* conflicted about Henry. My feelings for him are unclear. This situation is messy. I roll onto my side, set the alarm for 6:00 a.m., and pull the duvet over my head, happy to disappear for just a while longer.

It's the first day of class.

I'm sitting next to Henry and something feels off, as though I'm missing a limb.

I miss Jonathan. I wish he would return my calls. His lasting anger has cut me to the bone. I know I should just accept it if he needs space, however painful it is. After all, I kind of aggravated things by not talking during that explosive conversation. I check my phone yet again, hoping he's called or texted me, but he hasn't.

I think of that Beyoncé song, "Irreplaceable." In that song, she replaces her love with someone new, but that isn't my plan. Jonathan and I just need some time. We'll get past this and then we'll be fine, I just know it.

It also feels funny to be sitting in fashion school without Jake, but I know he's with me in spirit.

I peek at Henry from the corner of my eye: smooth cheeks, elegant demeanour, gorgeous smile. And beautiful clothes — he's always put together. Our school is located in Shanghai's Huaihai Road shopping area, and before class, Henry was carrying shopping bags to his locker. Not many students have the means to shop around here, including me.

How can he afford it? I don't know for sure. There's something really sleek about him, as though he doesn't want to show his true nature, the cracks under the designer armour. Kind of like the fashion industry itself, which, let's face it, can be superficial at times. Or is it just in Henry's nature to strive for perfection in every aspect of his life?

Maybe after school, I'll get him to talk. But first I'll have to apologize for running off yesterday.

As soon as Wei Lin, our digital media and technology teacher, walks into class, I forget all about men. I'm riveted by her look and her fierce attitude. She's roughly in her forties, and I know she's worked in the local fashion and media industries for years. She's the senior VP of one of the largest media companies in China, and also the fashion director of one of their popular websites. She stands tall and confident, sporting a razor-sharp bob, an avant-garde metallic jacket over a short black dress, slim trousers, and silver booties. She has real panache. I can't wait to hear her speak.

Henry sees my reaction and smiles. He knows this is why I came here: to get the inside scoop on the Chinese industry from the world's most renowned professionals, and to get some of their personal insights. This class is a stepping stone to my goals. I'm psyched.

Wei addresses the class in Mandarin first, introducing herself, her background, and the general topics that will be covered in class. She also explains some of the practical exercises we'll be doing, including visiting her offices and writing a piece for her website. She announces that the best articles will be selected for publication in her company's newsletter and on the website. This gets me totally lit up, and Henry nudges me, knowing how much that would mean to me. I grin and lift my coffee mug subtly in salute. I'm always up for a good writing challenge.

Wei then switches to English, as many of the students come from around the world. I take copious notes as she starts talking about digital communications, the importance of online branding, the different Chinese social media sites, and where the fashion media industry is going next.

She then addresses a topic that's on everyone's lips: Key Opinion Leaders, KOLs for short. This is the term used in China for what Westerners call "influencers." Given that I'm building my own online following, this subject interests me a lot. Eventually, I'd like to start trends on my own, particularly in eco-fashion and conscientious ways of shopping. I don't just want more followers; I want to influence change.

"KOLs have become a big part of any brand's checklist when operating in China. Their strong influence translates into massive earnings and income potential."

It's clear how important it is for a brand to work with KOLs right now. But will it last? Will the public realize that some of these so-called internet celebrities are being paid tons of money to push products on us? Some of them don't really do much to deserve the label of "celebrity," if you ask me … but maybe that's just sour grapes on my part.

"With so many KOLs now on the scene and the number increasing every day, luxury brands should consider more creative ways to work with those who inspire and a have loyal following," Wei says, making a sweeping hand gesture while she paces the front of the all-white classroom. She fits in perfectly with her surroundings. I'm totally inspired.

"KOLs have more influence on consumer behaviour and social trends than some of the biggest movie stars and singers in this country do. It's mind-boggling," Wei continues.

I think of Angelababy, one of the most famous KOLs in China, who has millions of social media followers. She collaborates with labels such as Dior and has graced the cover of the prestigious magazine *Madame Figaro*, among many others.

I turn to Henry. He's staring at the teacher with a look of awe on his face, as if he's learning something earth-shattering. Being an influencer himself, none of this should be a surprise to him. But it looks as though some kind of light bulb is going off in his head.

"There are Chinese KOLs in every imaginable field — not only fashion and sports, but also travel, pets, gardening, and food. Food is very popular right now."

She's right about that. I've already noticed several young Chinese women taking photos of their food in restaurants and cafés. Chinese social media sites like Weibo and WeChat are filled with pictures of tiny cakes, bowls of noodles, and designer coffees.

"But have we reached a stage of overreliance on KOLs?" the teacher asks rhetorically, while pacing back and forth. That was exactly what I was just wondering. "Perhaps. There's room to be more creative and expansive with publicity money. I think it should be more about collaboration, not just plain ads."

Yes! My thoughts exactly. I'm really getting into what Wei is saying.

"Some agencies that specialize in influencer marketing have over thirty-five thousand KOLs on their books — a huge number, which should sound alarm bells," she warns.

Henry has stopped taking notes completely. He's now staring at Wei with a look of disbelief, eyes bulging, mouth open. Again, I'm surprised. Shouldn't he know all of this? Why is he reacting this way? Maybe it's something to do with the business he's planning to launch?

"Brands need to prepare for when — not if — the KOL bubble bursts, like all bubbles do. The digital world is saturated with KOLs, each with millions of claimed follow-ers, and consumers may begin to tire of people being paid to prance around on their Weibo feeds for a particular brand."

That's exactly what I've been thinking! That's why I decided right from the start never to do paid or sponsored posts on *Bonjour Girl*. I wonder what Brian would think of her statements.

"So what should fashion businesses look for in the evo-lution of Chinese digital culture? It all comes back to qual-ity content." Wei sounds a lot like Maddie when she talks about these things. Her comments also remind me of last semester's lectures at Parsons about fashion and technology.

"In my work, I speak to many millennials in Shanghai, and their interest is in the rise and return of bloggers — not KOLs, not those who are paid to promote, but those who create original, honest content and share opinions based on genuine passions. People without Photoshopped facial features who write thoughtfully and express new and inter-esting ideas."

Wow. Okay, now I'm really excited. This validates all the effort and energy I've poured into my blog. I'm thrilled that I've kept at it.

I turn to face Henry, but he's gone. I was so immersed in what the teacher was saying that I didn't even notice him slipping away. Why did he leave? Something must have been bothering him. But what?

"Hey, you." I've managed to find Henry after class. He's sitting alone in a corner of the research centre, totally engrossed in something he's reading on his computer. It looks like an email. He still has a funny look on his face. "Why the disappearing act?"

"Sorry, Clementine, I had to scoot out to contact my business partner about something."

"Something to do with what the teacher said?"

"Uh, maybe. Not really."

Hmm. I'm not sure what kind of answer that is, but I let it go. He still hasn't turned to face me as he furiously types away.

"Should I come back later? Or meet you in the café? You seem … preoccupied."

"No, please wait! Just let me finish this message. I'll be done in a few minutes, I promise."

"Okay, take your time. I'll read some magazines while you finish."

This research centre is impressive. Not surprising, given that Condé Nast is the world's most prestigious fashion magazine publisher. The modern space is filled with gorgeous books, magazines, and other periodicals. I could spend hours reading in here. I'm in no rush to leave. I plop myself down on one of the low sofas and pick up a copy of *Vogue China*. Couldn't hurt to practise my Mandarin reading skills; they're pretty good, but they could always improve.

With a circulation of close to two million, *Vogue China* is one of the most successful fashion magazines on the continent. There's an article about the editor-in-chief, Angelica Cheung, who says that she always looks to the future and never dwells on the successes of the past. I like that idea.

I flip through the mesmerizing images of local fashion, taking in the colours and designs. There's an article about some of the best shops and cafés in the city — I note some of them on my phone.

One article in particular catches my eye. It's about the bookshops along Fuzhou Road that are a bibliophile's dream: large bookstores with cafés inside, teeny foreign shops with books in every imaginable language, specialty retailers dealing in art books or children's books, and used bookshops where you can flip through novels and wonder what the handwritten Mandarin notes mean. I definitely need to check these out.

My mouth gapes open at the image on the next page: it's Sandra, my fairy godmother from the friendly skies, dressed in a stunning black gown and shimmering jewels, with full makeup and a chic updo. *Wow.* When we met, she was wearing baggy travel clothes. In the photo, she's holding a plaque. As one of the philanthropists of the year, she's been nominated for an award. It says she's making an important contribution to the hospital where her sister is receiving care. Sandra in *Vogue*? Philanthropist of the year? This gives me goosebumps.

I knew Sandra was well off, but had no idea she was this wealthy. She flies coach and dresses simply. In addition to being smart and classy, she has a heart of gold, too. How lucky am I to have met her?

I stand up and ask the librarian to make a copy of the accompanying article. She kindly does it for me. I put it in my handbag for protection and good vibes, then sit back down to read some more while I wait for Henry.

He finally comes over, smiling and looking more relaxed. He's wearing his messenger bag across his chest.

"Sorry about that. I'm all yours now," he says slyly.

I know he expects a cheeky response, but I don't say anything. How do you respond to that?

He runs his fingers through his hair just like Jonathan does — it's something they have in common. He kneels down next to me to look at what I'm reading. At least, unlike Jonathan, he doesn't seem to remain in a funk for very long.

"Sorry about leaving class like that. I'm just putting a lot of time and resources into this online business of mine, and I want it to succeed."

The last time we discussed his projects, he'd said he was only at the planning stage. That's strange. "No problem. I get it," I whisper, trying to maintain the zen-like silence of the space.

"I have other people counting on me, too. There's a lot of pressure."

"Are your parents … helping you out?" I ask. I know I'm being nosy, but he's shared very little about his family thus far.

He looks away for a second with a pained expression. "My dad is no longer with us. He died over a decade ago."

"Oh, I'm so sorry, Henry."

"It's okay. I was going to tell you eventually."

"Illness?" As soon as I say it I know: not an illness. Much worse. I can see it in his face. I never should have asked. He bites his lip and looks away.

He takes a seat next to me. "He took his own life after the massive financial meltdown on Wall Street. He worked for one of the banks that went belly up. It killed his spirit."

I choke up listening to him. "I'm so sorry. That must have been horrible." I put my hand on his shoulder. I can feel his deep sadness. I guess I was right. Like all of us, he does have a story. I feel bad that I judged him as too intense. Could it be that he tries to maintain such a perfect outward appearance to hide the pain he's feeling inside?

"It was really tough. My mom especially had a hard time. That's when she moved back to Shanghai to be close to family. It's been challenging. I've been trying to focus on my dreams, but in the background, I always have this feeling of having been left behind by my dad. I'm trying to find my own way while also striving to make my dad proud."

I place my hand over his. I can relate to him on this level. I felt the same way when my mom left me and my dad to go on an international tour when I was only a toddler. I think that feeling of abandonment affects my ability to connect with others on a deep level. It's a continuous struggle.

"Wherever your dad is right now, I'm sure he is proud of you."

He looks at the floor.

"It's none of my business," I continue, "but whatever you do, you need to think about yourself, okay? Don't do it for him. Do it for *you*."

He looks up with tears in his eyes. The cracks in his designer armour are showing. It's kind of refreshing to see his vulnerable side.

He squeezes my hand tightly and lets his head fall on my shoulder while I finish reading the rest of the *Vogue China* in silence. Angelica Cheung is right: it's best to focus on the future, not dwell on the past.

Chapter Twenty-Three

IT'S BEEN A WEEK since the beginning of the summer semester and a little over a week since my disheartening exchange with Jonathan. Although I've tried to reach out many times since, he hasn't called back or responded to my texts. I've had a hard time sleeping or getting any work done. The situation is affecting my concentration. And it hurts. I wish I could just go over to his place and resolve this.

I do my best to push all this out of my mind as I head to my first class with Jean-Charles Luteau, a well-known fashion journalism guru from Paris.

"*Bonjour, Mademoiselle Liu,*" he says with that distinctive Parisian accent as I walk into class.

Jean-Charles Luteau is tall and slim, with dark-brown hair and a square jaw, and he's dressed in a sharp black suit. He's internationally renowned as an expert in fashion reporting and has been teaching here at Condé Nast for the last five years.

"*Bonjour, monsieur. Enchantée.*"

"I've heard about you and your work," he says.

"Oh." This takes me by surprise. "Do you know Maddie?"

"Yes, of course. I also know about your relation to her, but don't assume you'll receive preferential treatment because of it," he says dryly.

Ouch. His tone is cutting and a tad accusatory. I inhale deeply, reminding myself that I didn't get selected for this exchange program on the basis of my relationship to Maddie. I was selected by an independent committee based on merit and hard work.

"I don't operate under that assumption, Mr. Luteau. Quite the contrary. I prefer to have my work speak for itself."

"Well, speaking of that" — he zeroes in on me like a hawk — "I've read your blog, and I can't say your work speaks to me very much." He crosses his arms and leans against his desk. "Your recent posts are too commercial for my taste."

I remain frozen, feet planted in the doorway as other students walk past me. Most of them try to tiptoe around me in silence. They must see the shock on my face. Is Jean-Charles always like this?

I take a deep breath and remind myself that Parisians can be highly critical. But this does nothing to quell my insecurities.

"I respect your opinion, Mr. Luteau," I respond quietly. "I'd love to get some more specific feedback about my work when you have time."

He nods in response. "With pleasure."

"What was that about?" Henry whispers as I take a seat next to him.

"He doesn't like my work. We're off to a rocky start."

"Don't worry. He has a reputation for being tough on everybody. You'll survive."

"Sure I will. I made it through two semesters in New York, didn't I? Besides, everyone's entitled to their opinion," I whisper, trying to remain cool and mature about things. A few students send me sympathetic looks. I nod back appreciatively. We're all in this together.

"Today, we'll talk about the importance of solid storytelling," Jean-Charles announces. I sit up in my seat, trying to be optimistic, although I'm not sure how I'll manage to get through this class if I have such a serious handicap. Can he fail me just because he doesn't like my blog?

Jean-Charles begins by talking about his background as an editor at a prestigious French publication, then he talks about the critical importance of creating cohesive editorials. He presents a lengthy slideshow of the various features he's worked on over the years.

"In order to prove my point that digital storytelling is the future," he says, "I want you to partner with someone in this class, go out to the hallway, and create a short video with your phone about a product you love. It can be anything — clothing, accessories, beauty products — but choose wisely. The video must be engaging. Be back here in forty-five minutes."

Henry turns to me and grins. He's all smiles. He excels at this sort of thing. Making videos is his specialty.

"I have some ideas," he whispers and smiles, revealing his dimples.

"Great, because after what Jean-Charles said to me, I do not."

"No worries, I got this. Let's go." He nods toward the door as students begin to exit the classroom en masse.

I catch Jean-Charles looking at me from the corner of his eye. I can tell he's glaring at my outfit. I guess he doesn't approve of my apple-green sweatshirt, funky green-and-yellow banana skirt, and green-and-black high-heeled booties that I'm wearing with yellow socks. I'm a total rulebreaker here. Nobody here wears heels and socks, but I couldn't care less; it's a look I like and that I stand behind. I want to tell Jean-Charles that life should be spontaneous, interesting, and layered, and that's what I choose to reflect in my style of dress, but I can't see how it would do any good. He just doesn't get it.

"So, where are we going?" I ask Henry after he's fetched his backpack from his locker. He's also pulled out a large paper bag from a store whose name I don't recognize. It must be a local brand.

"Somewhere amazing."

"Okay, what's our product?"

"Ta-dah!" He pulls out a crisp white leather bag. It has a clean, boxy shape, and no logos or adornments.

"A friend of mine makes them. And she's been thriving — her bags sell like hotcakes."

"Cool. I really like how pristine it looks."

"Yeah, me too. Like a blank canvas." He grins. I have a feeling that his idea goes beyond a simple white bag.

He gently takes me by the elbow and leads me to the street, where he calls for a taxi.

"You're full of surprises," I say once we're in the back seat.

"You inspired me, Clementine!"

I can't help but smile. "Happy to hear I'm inspiring someone in that classroom," I say.

"Don't worry about Jean-Charles. He just needs some time to warm up to you."

"Yeah, right. I seriously doubt that'll happen anytime soon."

Henry nudges my elbow, and this time, his touch is electrifying. Sparks fly through my entire body. I roll down the window to get some (not so) fresh city air. I need to cool off. Peering out the window, I notice things I haven't before, like how some motorcyclists protect their legs, chests, and necks from the wind and the chill with funky-looking covers made of vivid multicoloured fabrics. There are different styles for men and women. It's a great concept. Why don't motorcyclists in Paris and New York do the same? Jake would get a real kick out of it. He'd probably design some himself.

Another thing that catches my eye is the people walking around town in their pyjamas. There are people shopping, drinking tea, walking around, and playing games in sleepwear — matching tops and bottoms in a bright array of bold colours and patterns. This makes me smile. I mean, why not?

Henry tells me this practice of stepping out in sleepwear started after the opening up of the country around 1980, when Western-style PJs started to be sold in China without proper instructions for use. Shanghai officials recently became so concerned about what effect this look might have on their city's cosmopolitan image that they ran a campaign about ten years ago to snuff out the fashion faux pas, posting signs saying *Pyjamas Don't Go Out the*

Door! The pyjama police even patrolled neighbourhoods, telling offenders to go home and change. Clearly, however, there are still people who resist. I'm all for it.

The taxi stops in front of a public market. Henry leads me to a young woman selling embroidered fabric swatches. They're intricate, bright, and cheery, and the colours take my breath away.

"These are Miao embroideries, traditional Chinese textiles from the southeast provinces," Henry explains. "Miao embroidery involves unique and complex stitches that give it a special look. The most common one is the satin stitch, which gives a shimmery effect. Choose the one you like most." I see that he's filming me with his phone as I make my selection.

"What is this for?"

"Take a guess," he says, holding up the white leather bag.

"Oh, I get it. We're customizing this bag now, are we?" I say with a posh English accent.

"Yes, darling."

"What a great idea! All righty, then."

I pick the swatch with the brightest pops of red. "These fabrics are stunning! They make me happy just looking at them," I say into the camera.

Then I smile at the young woman, who nods back. "You make these?" I ask in Mandarin, and she nods in the affirmative. "They're spectacular! You have so much talent."

I almost forget that I'm being filmed. I wrap two pieces of fabric around the white bag's handles. The effect is exquisite. I lift it up to show Henry. "Tradition and elaborate craftsmanship meets modern minimalism."

"Brilliant!"

I love this idea. It feels great to be creative. No matter what Jean-Charles thinks about me and my blog, I'm totally liking this class ... or is it Henry that I'm liking?

Henry pays for the fabric, then grabs my hand and pulls me away from the stand, through the countless market stalls, and eventually back to the street.

"What a great concept. You're so good at this stuff!"

"We're not done yet, Mademoiselle Liu."

"Oh?"

"The bag could use a bit more loving, don't you think?" he says, flashing his boyish grin.

"I guess. Do we have time?"

Henry looks at his watch. "Yes."

"Okay. Um, I think the bag needs some charms," I suggest.

"Good idea. And I know exactly where to find those."

"I really picked the perfect partner, didn't I? Oh, wait a minute, you picked me." I poke him. He pokes me back.

Henry hails a cab and asks the driver to take us to an address in the Tianzi Fang neighbourhood, an arts and crafts enclave in the French Concession.

We stop in front of a mall-like complex and enter a space where a young woman is at work creating jewellery. As we approach, I see that she's working on a pair of delicate earrings in the shapes of a flower and a bird.

"Clementine, meet Mia. She went to Condé Nast last year and launched her own jewellery line. She also lived in Los Angeles for a while, a few years ago. Clementine is studying in Shanghai for the summer," Henry says to Mia in English.

"It's lovely to meet you. I love these earrings. They're absolutely gorgeous," I tell her.

"Thank you. I hope you're enjoying our city so far."

"Yes, very much."

"We're here for a project for our journalism class," Henry explains. "Creating a visual story. We're looking to add some original accessories to this bag, and we'd like to add yours. What do you say?" he asks.

Mia immediately perks up. "Oh, of course. Is this for Jean-Charles's class?" she asks. I think back again to his comments about my blog. My embarrassment must show on my face, because she says, "Don't worry about him, Clementine. Jean-Charles can be a little salty."

"Yeah, I've noticed."

But I am glad I'm not the only one who's noticed.

"Go ahead, Clementine," says Henry, "select the piece you think would look best on our bag."

He films me as I reach for a pair of chandelier earrings in the shapes of lotus flowers. I attach the earrings to the bag handles, where they contrast nicely against the bold artisanal fabric. Our bag looks marvelous now, like a high-end luxury designer handbag.

"Thanks, Mia," Henry says, paying her for the earrings. "You'll get credit for this in our video, and some free publicity in class, I promise!" He gives her a peck on the cheek.

"It's my pleasure! Lovely to meet you, Clementine." She waves as we rush away. We've got to hurry back to class.

Before we hop in a cab, Henry stops at a roadside stall to grab a bouquet of lilies, which he places inside the bag — the effect is breathtaking. The plain white bag has been completely transformed and beautified.

In the cab, on the way back to school, Henry films me holding the bag and explaining our creative process.

Henry finishes with salesy-sounding slogan. "This bag is a blank canvas that transforms the ordinary into the delightful, wherever it goes."

"Aw, that's sweet, but please don't put that in the video," I say jokingly. "I don't want to ruin it."

Everyone else is already assembled in the classroom when we hurry in. Jean-Charles gives us a cold stare.

"You guys are late."

"Sorry, we were stuck in traffic —" Henry starts.

"Traffic? Couldn't you have created your video here on campus, like the rest of your classmates? Is Condé Nast not good enough for you?"

Merde.

Henry's getting an earful and he doesn't deserve it. Obviously Jean-Charles dislikes me and is just taking it out on my poor friend.

"It was my idea," I say, taking the blame. The teacher just smirks.

"Okay, Ms. Liu. Since your team was the last to show up, you'll be the first to show us your work."

I tense up. I'm starting to have doubts about our video. I have a feeling it's going to be strongly criticized. A part of me wants to run out into the street and start again.

My heart pounding in my chest, I hand over Henry's phone so that Jean-Charles can plug it into the projector. The video begins, and we see shots of Henry's hand holding the white bag amidst the stalls of the public market. Then, his hand holds the bag up in front of the Miao embroideries, before the camera zooms in on the actual textiles. So far, so good, I think; the effect is powerful. We're showcasing traditional textiles and local artisans. I can see from our classmates' reactions that they approve of the angle we took.

We see a close-up of me picking out the colourful swatches, then looping them through the bag's handles. I cringe and try not to look over at our teacher. I don't want to see his reaction.

The next scene is of me entering a taxi, then some Shanghai street scenes filmed through the window. Henry has even added some cool background music using an app on his phone — when did he have time to do that? I'm amazed. It looks really good. The camera follows me walking into Mia's boutique, where we pick out the earrings. From the corner of my eye, I detect a smile on Jean-Charles's face. He must think highly of Mia, one of his former students. Bless her and her talent — she's probably just saved us. The video ends with Henry picking the bouquet of lilies and placing them in the bag, and then a close-up of my feet walking into class.

I think we aced it. Henry wears a satisfied grin.

But my feeling of joy comes crashing down as soon as Jean-Charles opens his mouth.

"Interesting concept, but poorly executed. Way too bland and predictable," he says, looking mostly in my direction. "Boring, boring, boring."

Too bland? Boring? We picked out colourful embroideries and intricate jewellery made by talented artisans. We drove around the city to make it happen! I stay quiet, trying to keep calm. I wish I could run out of class and call Jonathan. I miss his support, his kind words, his loving presence.

"It's a bit clichéd. It's been done time and time again, that visit to the local market thing," he says, rolling his eyes, his arms still crossed over his chest. "Nice try, though. Next time, rather than wasting your energy running around Shanghai, stay closer to school and focus on being more creative, *d'accord*?"

Ouch. I look over at Henry. He looks completely downtrodden. He just stares at the desk and nods in silence.

"Does anyone else have any comments?" the teacher asks the class.

One kind soul raises her hand. "I really like how they incorporated the jewellery made by a local artisan. Those jewels sparkled against the white bag. The effect was magical. I like how the video represents the past, the present, and the future of Chinese fashion."

"*Oui, oui*, you're right, the jewels are probably the one saving grace," Jean-Charles admits, uncrossing his arms and removing Henry's phone from the overhead projector.

Geez, the only saving grace? I try to look on the bright side: adding the charms was my idea. Nevertheless, earning this teacher's approval is going to be an uphill battle.

That was a tough lesson in humility, I think on my way home. Henry and I weren't in a talkative mood after class, so we went our separate ways. On the subway, I begin questioning my creative journey. Is what I'm doing of any value? Am I wasting my time, blogging? Jean-Charles has planted a kernel of doubt in my mind. Should I change *Bonjour Girl*? And if so, how? Whereas Brian thinks I should go more commercial, Jean-Charles thinks I'm already too much so. What direction should I take? More importantly, should I listen to either of them?

After sulking for a good half hour, I notice an elderly lady sitting across from me. She must be in her eighties, at least. She's sitting serenely, holding her cane in one hand and her handbag in the other, wearing a colourful dress under a bland-looking raincoat. She looks at me with a glint in her eye, like she knows something.

Suddenly, I relax. Would this peaceful woman across from me get all tied up in knots over some teacher's opinion of her work? Definitely not. I smile at her appreciatively.

Regardless of what Jean-Charles thinks, I have a loyal readership, and some teachers back home like what I do just fine.

I pick up my phone to message Henry.

Feeling bruised. You?

No kidding. I've never had such negative comments about my work before.
It was pretty humiliating. I feel like a
gigantic loser.

You're no loser! It's only his opinion.
Other people liked our video. I've been
through worse than this. I was cyber-
bullied in New York last semester.

Really? Why didn't you tell me about it?

I've been trying to get over it and
move on. It was a fellow student.
She was expelled.

I'm sorry, Clementine. You don't
deserve crap like that.

Nobody does. It's awful. It makes
you feel so small.

Like what Jean-Charles did
to us today?

Much worse. He was just criticizing
our work. He didn't attack our integrity,
character, or self-worth.

Speak for yourself, girl!

Lol. Try to get some sleep, you'll forget
all about it in the morning.

I hope so. There must be a lesson
in all of this.

Yeah, it's that we can't always be
the favourite. We can't always
be number one.

I guess …

Anyway, *I* loved our video and
your ideas. I thought the whole
concept was fabulous.

Thanks, Clementine. Good night and
sweet dreams XO

Good night, partner. See you tomorrow
X

I can't believe I'm the one giving Henry a pep talk.
I guess being bullied last fall has made me stronger and
wiser. I've developed a thicker skin. Thanks to Parsons in
New York, I've learned to own my work and my art, or at
least attempt to do so. Thanks to Condé Nast in Shanghai,
I'm learning to take it all in stride.

Chapter Twenty-Four

ACCORDING TO THE AUTHOR Dodie Smith, family is "that dear octopus from whose tentacles we never quite escape, nor, in our inmost hearts, ever quite wish to." I realize how true this is on Sunday morning as I walk into a dim sum restaurant on the busy Dingxi Road in the Changning District to meet my entire Chinese extended family for brunch. Luckily, I took some time to meditate and have a quiet coffee at my favourite café this morning first. I needed a moment to relax and unwind, and get over Jean-Charles's negativity. I'm trying hard to let go of it, but I still feel the sting. While I sipped my cappuccino, I kept repeating to myself the advice that I gave Henry, as well as the old saying *Sticks and stones may break my bones, but words will never hurt me.* It worked — I left the coffee shop feeling rejuvenated and ready to mingle and practise my Mandarin.

My cousin Becky jumps up from her seat to meet me just inside the entrance. "Oh, Clementine, we're so happy you're here!"

I look over at the table — there must be at least twenty people sitting there, most of whom I've never met. I inhale deeply and brace myself for a noisy meal and, most likely, some nosy questions, too. I may not have met them all, but I know my relatives.

My father's sister, Jiao, which means "dainty and lovely," was the one who organized this reunion, and I'm grateful to her. I get along well with my cousins, and I'm excited to get to see them in their own city. Jiao's family and her kids used to stay with us in Paris every year; I always looked forward to their visits. On those trips, she would always take me and her daughters shopping, then to some museum exhibit or other, and finally, to lunch. I remember eating *mousse au chocolat* with my cousins.

Jiao wears her name well; she's petite with elegant taste, just like my dad. She's younger than my father, and he's always taken care of her fondly. Having overcome a difficult childhood with their highly controlling father, they now both appreciate spending time together in peace.

"Hello, Becky! You look amazing!" I say in Mandarin, marvelling at how much my cousin has grown since I last saw her. She looks like a woman now. She's wearing a black dress with chic stockings, and her face is nicely made up with black liquid eyeliner and red lipstick. She doesn't look anything like the athletic sweatpants-wearing teenager she used to be.

She kisses me on the cheek, and I hug her back.

"Thanks! So do you!" she says, looking at my ensemble. I've toned down my quirky style a few notches for this family affair. I'm wearing a feminine gingham dress with a ruffle hem that I found in a flea market in Brooklyn, along with a jean jacket and my red booties. I had hoped to avoid the usual side stares, but I can tell from the look on my aunt's face that she's surprised by what I'm wearing. It's far from conventional or conservative. I know she'd never be caught dead in this outfit, but I don't care. It's who I am, and your family is supposed to accept you just the way you are, isn't it?

I walk up to the table and shake hands with my other cousins, Emily, Ming, and Vince, my Uncle Jaw-Long, and some of his brothers, sisters, and their kids. Everyone is smiling and welcoming me as I take a seat at the round table.

Then question period begins.

"So … what exactly are you studying in Shanghai?" my uncle begins. The server comes over with a fresh teapot just then, as if he knows that I'm going to need to clear my throat a lot. I take a sip before responding. My uncle's the corporate type, a manager at a large insurance company, so this conversation may go off the rails.

"I'm studying fashion at the Condé Nast Center of Fashion & Design. It's affiliated with a large international publishing company." My cousin Becky's eyes light up. Clearly, she reads *Vogue China* and knows what I'm talking about. Other family members just give me funny looks.

"I'm taking online media and marketing classes. It's a summer program, and teachers from all over the world come to share their specialized knowledge. I love it so far." I leave out the Jean-Charles Luteau bit.

"It sounds intriguing," my uncle says, waving the server over.

He orders the food, including prawns, crispy duck, and a ton of dumplings. I can tell by how much he's ordering that it's going to be a very long brunch. I just hope the questioning doesn't last the entire time.

"So, why fashion, Clementine?" my uncle's sister asks me. "Why not medical school or law school? You're so smart! And your parents have money to send you to the best schools."

I mentally roll my eyes and take a deep breath. "I am going to a good school. Parsons is one of the top fashion schools in the world. It's at the forefront of innovation and fashion technology." I hope this will end things right here.

Alas, it does not.

"Fashion technology? Is that important?" my uncle asks. "What about real technology, like Amazon or Google? Those types of companies pay for their employees' food and other good perks."

"Really? That would be a great place for you," my aunt says to her son, Vince.

"Yes, I'm sure those are great places to work, but that's not my interest," I respond, trying to stay calm and collected. My uncle's name means "like a dragon," and now I see that it suits him.

For a moment, I'm grateful that I have an artist mother, no matter what her shortcomings are, as well as a supportive father who's always encouraged me to pursue my passions and dreams. They've always been open-minded.

"Why not?" my uncle presses.

"Well, because I'm passionate about fashion. I always have been, ever since I was a young girl, and probably always will be."

"Yes, that's very true," my Aunt Jiao concedes, giving me a kind, knowing look. "I remember Clementine playing dress-up with her mother's stage costumes." She smiles, taking some of the pressure off. Finally, we're getting somewhere. I make a mental note to try to change seats so I can sit next to her for dessert.

"I've also started a blog called *Bonjour Girl*. I interview people who make a difference in the fashion industry or in the world at large, and I have a pretty decent following," I say proudly. "Becky knows about it." My cousin nods enthusiastically. I wonder if Becky will end up pursuing her own dreams and aspirations, or if her father will decide her path for her. I have my suspicions.

"Can you make money doing this blogging thing?" my uncle's sister asks, annoyingly. "Is the fashion industry able to pay you? It seems more like a hobby to me."

My other cousin, Emily, finally chimes in. "Of course she can make money blogging! She can make loads of it, too. Haven't you heard about these bloggers with massive followings who are making a killing on Weibo and WeChat?" I mentally high-five her.

"If you say so."

Some of the food arrives, giving me a breather. I guess the whole follow-your-dreams movement hasn't reached some of my extended family members yet.

"You could build a fashion media empire," my cousin Vince says, grinning as he digs into a pork bun. "Now, that's how you become rich!" Clearly he's following in his father's footsteps. He's going to business school next year, presumably to do just that.

"No thanks. That's not my dream."

"What do you love most about fashion?" my aunt asks between bites.

"I'm really interested in sustainability — promoting diversity and brands that want to protect the environment and make a difference in this world. That's the sort of thing I like to talk about on my blog."

Silence. Blank stares. Everyone just looks at me. I bite into a dumpling, trying to ignore the awkwardness.

They just don't get it, but that's okay, they don't have to. Besides, I'm getting used to it. I guess I need to learn to stand up for my opinions and what I think is right.

Near the end of the meal, when the sweet dishes have been brought out, I take my cup of tea to the other side of the table and sit between Jiao and Becky. Their warm reception makes me feel better.

"I'm so proud of you, Clementine," Jiao says, "for doing what you love. Don't listen to your uncle — he's so old-fashioned about these things. And he can be difficult, just like your grandfather was. He thinks that money is the only measure of happiness and success. I understand what you're doing, and I'm impressed by your determination." I nod and give her a hug. "I've been following you on WeChat," she says.

"Thank you, Aunt Jiao, I really needed to hear that today."

"You will go far, my dear. You have class and tact. Unlike your mother," she adds with disdain.

Oh boy, here we go. My aunt has never liked my mother much. She always resented the fact that my dad married a foreign diva with an attitude, especially since that diva turned out to also have a penchant for other, younger men. I stay silent. I don't want to get into it right now.

"I always thought your dad should've married that nice Chinese girl he was dating in college," she mutters. I want to respond that if he had, I wouldn't be here, but instead just drop it. After a brief catch-up with my cousins about their studies and dating lives, I take my cup of tea and head back to the other side of the table. I'll take an honest discussion about the merits of fashion school over petty gossip any day.

Chapter Twenty-Five

"DID YOU KNOW THAT in certain parts of China, India, and Indonesia, residents can predict fashion trends merely by looking at the colour of the water in nearby rivers?" Henry asks the large crowd. The room goes quiet and there are a couple of gasps. I'm excited for him — several hundred people are squeezed into this room for his panel discussion today, which confirms how relevant this conversation is right now. Fashion students really do care about the future of our planet, and it's exciting to see.

Henry is looking confident in a pressed white shirt, black pants, polished black loafers, and red argyle socks. He reminds me of Maddie when she leads panels at Parsons. I know she'd be thrilled to see me sitting here. Thanks to Henry, I'm in the front row.

He's interviewing the creators of a documentary about the effects of fashion on rivers worldwide. A large screen set up high above his head is looping a sequence of shots of unnaturally blue water flowing through villages around the world. It's an alarming sight. The blue dye comes from the manufacturing of blue jeans, which are worn by at least half the world's population. If only consumers knew about this. I'm proud of Henry for sharing this important message. Thanks to the filmmakers and talks like this, more people are learning about this kind of pollution, and this might convince them to shop more conscientiously.

I recently watched a TED Talk by an activist who admitted to owning more than twenty-five pairs of jeans. She said she hadn't been fully aware that she had bought so many. "Who needs so much?" she asked the audience. The answer is no one. I feel good about doing my part; I hardly ever wear jeans.

Louder gasps fill the room as Henry points to the images of polluted rivers and oceans. The strong reaction is no surprise since China is the largest manufacturer of clothing on the planet, including blue jeans. Sadly, this means that China produces vast amounts of pollution, too. The good news is that the students gathered here today will become the decision makers of tomorrow and agents of social change, so their reaction gives me hope.

Henry looks my way and flashes his boyish grin.

The young woman sitting next to me catches this exchange and smiles. She probably assumes there's something going on between us. I quickly look down at my phone and pretend I haven't noticed, then cover my bare shoulders with the light-pink silk shawl I picked up yesterday at an outdoor market on my way home from brunch.

I busy myself by snapping a photo of the stage with my phone, catching the polluted blue rivers in the background, and post it to my WeChat account.

Attending a terrific panel hosted by
Conde Nast in Shanghai. I'm in a
#bluemood learning about #blueriv-
ers caused by #toomanybluejeans
#Shopconsciously

"If you care about water quality and ethical textile production, then this is a project worth supporting," Henry
says as the two documentarists take their seats. "Thank
you, John and Lisa, for visiting Shanghai to talk about your
film. We're thrilled to have you here. Can you please tell us
what motivated the making of it?"

"Sure," Lisa replies. "It's a hard truth to swallow, but
fashion is killing the planet and, more specifically, the
world's rivers. They're becoming extremely polluted, more
so every single day, as textile manufacturers dump waste
water directly into nearby waterways. The denim industry
is particularly destructive, as it uses a toxic mix of chemicals to create the jeans we all love. We've come to China
to help spread the word with the objective of creating
change."

Lisa's answer makes me smile. This is why I applied to
fashion school in the first place. I want to make a difference,
too. I'd far rather talk about issues like this on *Bonjour Girl*
than write traditional fashion editorials. I wish Brian had
never put any doubt in my mind.

"No one wants to buy a shirt that someone died to
make," John says, referring to the building collapse in
Bangladesh a few years ago that killed thousands of gar-
ment workers. "But what about a pair of jeans that are
destroying and polluting our planet?"

"For most people, it doesn't register because it's happening far from their homes," Henry adds, "but it should, considering how many villages rely on this water. The pollution also causes widespread illness." I sit up in my chair. I'm so proud of him. "China produces huge amounts of textiles, and this country is facing massive ecological disaster."

The conversation goes on for a solid thirty minutes, Henry leading the panel with tact, intelligence, and thoughtful questions. From time to time, he looks my way with that luminous smile. Why does he have to be so damn attractive?

He opens the floor to questions, and dozens of hands go up. It's obvious these students are interested in sustainability, ethics, and the environment. I share some of their questions on social media as I follow along.

When I raise my hand, I feel several hundred pairs of eyes on me. This is my big coming out at the Condé Nast Fashion Center.

"Given the widespread use of chemicals in the fashion industry, what prompted you to use the manufacturing of blue jeans as the focal point of your documentary?"

The girl sitting next to me gives me an approving nod.

"I'm glad you asked," Lisa responds. "When I started my research, I came across an image of the Pearl River here in China as seen from space. You could see that the river had turned blue. It was indigo-blue, and I thought to myself, 'Oh dear, it's the ever-popular blue jeans.'"

"Blue jeans are that iconic item that everybody owns, but as we've seen, they're actually a problem," says John.

After the question period, Henry stands in the middle of the stage, full of confidence and swagger. He has clearly gotten over the negative comments we received from Jean-Charles Luteau. He thanks the guests and the audience, then adds that he has an announcement.

"If you appreciate this type of content, there's an online resource I'd like to talk to you about." He looks my way out of the corner of his eye.

Is he about to ... No, please no, don't do that ...

I shrink in my seat, waiting for him to call out my name and mention *Bonjour Girl*. After what happened with Stella last semester, I really don't like attracting attention to myself. It'll only end up causing some kind of trouble, which I want to avoid at all costs.

I pull my baseball cap lower on my head and cross my arms. I didn't ask for him to bring it up. I mean, first the over-the-top video, then the surprise welcome at the airport, the expensive blouse, and now this. It's a bit much.

"You can read more about the impact of the fashion industry on the planet on my new website, *Eco-Couture!*"

It takes a second for me to register what he has said. I look up at the stage — now he's avoiding my eye.

Did I hear correctly? Henry is launching his own website? My eyes bulge and my jaw goes slack. Where did that come from?

"I've been working on this new site for several months now, and I'm excited to tell you about it today. For more information, you can check us out online or talk to me. I look forward to having you with us on this new journey ..."

On the screen overhead, his website appears. The graphic design is quite polished and impressive; it's the sort of slick design that makes *Bonjour Girl* look pretty damn boring. His friend Stephen walks up on stage and begins to display all kinds of fancy videos and other impressive bells and whistles that appear on their new platform. My mouth goes dry. Maybe I should hire Stephen as a consultant so that he can upgrade *Bonjour Girl* with all of this stuff?

The young woman sitting next to me gets up and immediately goes up to Henry to find out more. He already has a fan. As for me, I'm at a complete loss for words. He said he was planning to launch an NGO or a branding agency, not a website. What the hell is going on?

My mind spins. Is this why he's been asking me so many questions about *Bonjour Girl*?

I almost laugh. Well, it's not like I had the monopoly on ethical fashion blogs, did I?

He sees me standing there with my mouth wide open and brushes past his fans and over to me.

"What did you think?"

"The panel was awesome. The announcement … a bit unexpected. Why didn't you say something about it before?"

"I wanted to surprise you." He gives me a worried look.

"You certainly did. I mean, what you're doing is terrific, don't get me wrong. I like the concept — obviously, I do. It's just … we're friends, aren't we? Don't friends tell each other about these things?"

Jake would never keep something like this from me.

"I'm sorry." Henry puts his hand on my shoulder. "I don't want you to think that I'd hide anything from you. I was so excited to share this. I'm in awe of you. You're an inspiration to me. You know that, right?" He gazes deep into my eyes with a smoldering look that makes my knees go weak. His eyes are pleading with me to believe him.

I shrug and sigh. "It's okay. You wanted to do a *grand dévoilement*, I get it. I'm happy for you," I finally say. "I'm impressed with your graphics. You can count on me being a loyal reader."

"Impressed, or super mega impressed?" he asks, putting his hands on his hips and grinning.

"Both," I say, knowing it's what he wants to hear.

He responds by kissing me on the cheek. My face burns.

Then he reaches for my arm and leads me toward the stage. "Come on, I want you to meet the filmmakers."

"Oh, great. I'd love to interview them for *Bonjour Girl*."

He stops in his tracks and gives me a funny look. "Oh, well, I was hoping to have an exclusive interview for my site," he says, completely serious.

I take a step back. Since when do bloggers claim exclusivity on their content and interviews? Especially bloggers who are supposedly friends?

"I'm sorry," he says. "I don't mean to offend you. But you know how important exclusive content can be when you first launch, right?"

"Sure, I understand," I mutter.

But do I really?

Chapter Twenty-Six

JUST WHEN YOU think you have a person figured out, they surprise you in more ways than one.

Henry and I and two of his friends from school are all sitting in a subway car after the panel discussion. Masha and Lilian are both studying fashion marketing, and they seem to be in complete admiration of Henry and his big plans.

I look on as he chats up the girls, talking animatedly about his new website. I can't say I blame them; he's nice to look at, he's convincing, and his intentions of saving the planet are admirable. He mentions his friend Stephen, who'll be the technical genius behind the scenes, and his intention to launch advertising campaigns all over Chinese social media and to get local celebrities and NGOs to endorse the site.

It all sounds impressive. So why am I feeling so put out by it? Probably because these are the very things I'd like to do with my own blog, but can't afford to right now. Although I've amassed a solid following, I'll need many more page views and subscribers before I can invest in new technologies and advertising.

I sit quietly across from the other three, watching the scene with detachment. Henry's lapping up all the attention. I can also tell he's trying to make me jealous of these girls, but it's not working. He's being far too obvious, I'm still miffed about the whole *Eco-Couture* thing, and I have an amazing boyfriend back home. At least I hope I do. I still haven't been able to get through to Jonathan.

I try to snap myself out of this mood and put on a happy face. Apparently, we're going somewhere fun, and I don't want to bring down the vibe. Henry has been such a good host so far, I don't want to spoil our friendship over a spat about blogging. Maybe that's one of the lessons I needed to learn: it really isn't a race to the top.

My dad once told me about the importance of being a good sport, in all areas of life. Support the plans and successes of others, and that goodwill will always come back to you in spades.

"So, where are we going?" I ask, interrupting their conversation. I can tell Henry is relieved that I've finally said something.

"We're going somewhere supremely Shanghaiesque."

"Is there a dress code? Do I need to change?" I look down at what I'm wearing: bright-blue palazzo pants, a kimono-style jacket with red-and-blue embroidered silk bird motifs and delicate ribbons at the collar, and the navy-blue baseball hat I got on a street corner in New York. I'm also wearing some funky white booties that I got on sale before leaving the U.S. They give my look an avant-garde feel.

"Of course not. You look amazing and on point, as always," Henry says. The two women stare at me. As fashion school students, being complimented on the way you dress is the ultimate feedback.

We get out at the station closest to Zhaojibang Road and walk a few blocks, with Henry leading the way. This gives me the chance to talk with Masha and Lilian, who, Henry has told me, both love a lot of the same things I do: vintage shopping, books, doing research for school projects, and romantic comedies.

One of them actually spent a year in Paris as an intern at the same magazine I worked for, so we gossip about some people we both know.

Eventually, Henry stops in front a tall building where the words Haoledi KTV flash before my eyes.

I've heard of KTV, or karaoke television, a high-end kind of karaoke with private rooms, high-tech tablets for picking songs, loudspeakers, comfortable sofas, and mood lighting. These bars are super popular here. I've also seen videos of my relatives at KTV bars, looking and sounding foolish as they sing songs by people like Mariah Carey. But they don't seem to care, which is the best part.

"Karaoke? Really?" I poke Henry playfully.

"Sure, why not?" He pokes me back.

"Because I can't sing, that's why! I sound like a wailing cat."

"Do you think most people in there can? It's about loosening up and kicking back with friends."

"Let's go in, then!"

"Yeah!" Lilian yelps, twirling on the sidewalk, her rainbow-coloured trench coat floating in the wind.

Henry grabs me by the hand and leads me inside. It's like a cross between a hip nightclub and Disneyland. There are costumed hostesses, thumping music, elaborate drinks menus, and private rooms, each with its own theme and decor. Karaoke in Shanghai isn't like in New York, where the entire bar can hear your pathetic performance. Thank god for that.

"I booked this room especially for you," Henry says.

As soon as we walk in, I understand what he means. There are pink Marie Antoinette–style sofas and dreamy illustrations of hot air balloons on the walls. Low coffee tables hold magazines and candles and funky drink holders.

I think of Jonathan and how much he loves going out. He'd love this place. I try not to think about him too much, though — it'll only make me feel bad again. I think of Jake instead, and of how much *he'd* love to be here. I can picture him doing his thing to some old Destiny's Child song. I feel a pang in my stomach, a deep yearning for him and his bold presence. But this is no time to be sad.

I look up at Henry, and he grins proudly. He knows he's scored major points by selecting this room. I take a seat on a hot-pink sofa while he begins to set up the system.

"Start thinking of a song, Clementine. You'll be up soon."

I give him a pleading look. "No way!"

"Yes way, you're our guest star, and it's your first time at KTV."

"Come on, are you kidding me? You're the one who likes being in the spotlight, not me," I shoot back.

"All right, then." He does a few sound checks to some Katy Perry song, and we all start to get in a fun mood.

Lilian hands me the drinks menu.

"What are you having?" I ask her.

"A Tsingtao."

"Okay, I'll have one, too." I remind myself to go slow on the drinking, remembering again that time I ended up pole dancing in a nightclub. This is no time for a repeat performance.

As soon as the machine is set up, Masha gets up from the pink sofa, her flowy purple shirt floating behind her.

"I'm going first!" she announces, saving me.

The waitress brings our drinks, Henry sits down in the middle of the pink sofa, and we prepare for Masha's performance. I can tell it's going to be epic; she's getting into it, rolling her neck like a boxer before a match, shaking out her arms and legs as though she's going to fully embody the star she's about to cover.

She picks "Simply the Best" by Tina Turner.

The song begins and Masha twirls her small hips around, kicks her heels, and shakes her head like Tina Turner. She belts out the lyrics with such gusto and conviction — I'm in awe of her moves *and* her singing skills. I pump my fist in the air to punctuate that part about being better than all the rest.

"She really is the best!" I say to Henry over the loud music.

He shakes his head and bends over my ear. "You are." The words float into my ears, as though suspended in mid-air. Feeling his lips beside my ear sends a frisson of desire throughout my entire body. Unable to move, I just sit there while Henry's words, Tina Turner's lyrics, and Masha's singing blur together.

After Masha finishes her spectacular performance, I wake up from my trance and give her the standing ovation she deserves — we all do. Her faces lights up.

"You're amazing!" I give her a hug. "You belong on stage!"

She covers her face with her hands shyly, as if she doesn't realize the power of her stage presence. "Thank you."

"It's the truth! You rock!"

I sit back down and take a few sips of my beer while Henry picks up the mike. He seems to have forgotten his plans to rush me onstage, thank goodness. Masha is a tough act to follow, but that doesn't seem to faze him. He picks "Purple Rain" by Prince, a surprising choice. Can he sing that high? He begins shaking his hips in an unexpectedly sexy way.

The way Henry sways to the music sets my mind and body spinning. He sings so well, it blows my mind. I think of the gorgeous video he created for me before I arrived, the care he took to make sure I arrived safely at my apartment, the kindness he showed in introducing me to his friends and classmates, his impressive creativity, the way he took charge of the eco-fashion panel with his commanding presence, and the vulnerability he showed in opening up about his father.

He holds my gaze. The alcohol is making me lose my inhibitions. I begin to dance beside to the sofa. Masha dims the lights and encourages me to take off my shoes. All three of us sing along with Henry, dancing in the Purple Rain.

After an impressive finish, Henry takes a bow, and my two new female friends lift their beers high above their heads. Henry walks past them toward me.

"So what did you think?"

"It was stupendous."

He grins. My knees go weak.

I take a last sip of my beer and tell everyone that I need to leave. I'm facing a slippery slope. I can feel my resolve melting and my attraction growing by the minute.

Henry follows me out the door and into the street. "Why are you leaving so soon? I organized this whole night just for you …"

I just stare at him blankly. What am I doing? Guilt washes over me. Did I purposely create distance from Jonathan to make room for this? Or was it the other way around — did Jonathan push me away? If I did it, then what's wrong with me?

I put my hands over my face, unable to look at Henry. He removes my hands slowly, places his hands on my cheeks, and looks at me for a long moment. A scooter rushes past us and hits the curb, sending me sprawling into Henry's arms. I linger there for a moment, then he kisses me, right there in the middle of the sidewalk in front of the KTV bar. My blood is pumping fast. I let myself melt in his arms, feeling both elated and conflicted. It's a bitter-sweet feeling, but delicious at the same time.

Chapter Twenty-Seven

I OPEN MY EYES, then shut them again. Sunlight is peering through my bedroom blinds, but I can't face the day just yet. I try to brush away the memory of last night, but I can't. I feel elated, ashamed, and confused. Nothing makes sense.

I stretch out my arms, jump out of bed, and go to the window. As I look out over the plane trees, I see people strolling through the park and a young couple kissing on a bench below. Shanghai really is the Paris of the East, inspiring romance all around.

I remember Sandra's words. *You will know. You will just know.*

But the truth is, I just don't know.

I shower. Usually, I get strong insights under the flowing hot water, but not today. All I can think about is Henry, Prince, and "Purple Rain." My mind wanders back to the kiss and how painful it was to extricate myself from, because it was, well, so damn good. I did manage to pull away when a taxi stopped in front of us. Henry tried to pull me back toward him, but I just had to go. And now I'm swimming in remorse.

I put on a bright-yellow peasant blouse with pink and blue embroidered flowers and a pair of flowy paisley pants. After a quick breakfast, I decide to write a post for *Bonjour Girl*. It's time to get back to blogging more consistently. It'll help me get my mind off of things, at least for a while.

Brian's advice about thinking outside the box keeps replaying in the back of my mind, and so does Henry's. Maybe they're both right: I should be more open to other people's suggestions. What thought-provoking local topic could I write about? What would my friends back home like to read about?

After staring out the window for a few more minutes, I get a flash of an idea. What about a New York vs. Shanghai story, comparing and contrasting the two different cultures and their fashion styles? Shanghai fashionistas are quickly becoming much bolder in the way they dress. It's all very exciting. It would be fun to highlight these differences.

I begin by looking at pictures on my phone of young women in New York, including some of the highly colourful characters I've come across on my many afternoon walks in Central Park. My favourite pastime is checking out and taking pictures of cool streetwear. That's where I find the best style inspiration, both for myself and for my blog.

One photo catches my eye: a young woman dressed in black with high platform shoes, purple leggings, and matching hair. In another, a young couple with lavender and pink hair stroll arm in arm. They're wearing pastel colours — yellow shorts, striped pink shirts, and lime-green socks — and looking like a double scoop of sorbet. They were a sight to behold. I draft some commentary about each of the photographs.

I find another picture on my phone that I'd almost forgotten about. It's a selfie I took with the young woman I met in the women's change room at the Song Liung boutique. She was trying on this magnificent dress by Victoire & Sophie, a famous Parisian designer. After we exchanged pleasantries and took our picture together, Henry told me that the French designer is planning a runway show in Shanghai in a few weeks. It's going to be a mega multimillion-dollar production, with tons of local celebrities, media, and fashionistas. He also suggested that I might get invited to the event if I post something about them on *Bonjour Girl* with links to their page.

I've heard of this label. I've also read about how one of the designers has a reputation for being gauche on social media, so I'm a little hesitant to post anything about their work, but since both Brian and Henry have suggested linking to designers on my blog, and because that woman's dress really *was* spectacular, I decide to hop on the bandwagon and promote their upcoming presence in Shanghai. I send an email to the head of their marketing team in Paris to see if they'd be willing to pay me for affiliated links and draft a caption for the photo so I can add it to my post.

Then I add some photos from my shopping trip with Henry, including one of Mark at Song Liung and one of Julia and Ting at Annata, and write some text about them, too, discussing how the cultures of New York and Shanghai appreciate each other's style of dress.

I notice a notification on my phone. It's Henry on WeChat, wondering if I have time to meet up. Remorse bubbles up to the surface. I wish that kiss had never happened — I don't want to lose him as a friend. That would be a major loss. I ignore his message for now. I'm in the middle of writing. And one thing I know for sure is that when you discover your passion and purpose, it's like being in love. Nothing and no one can distract you from the object of your professional affection, even when your mind is still buzzing.

I'm knee-deep in a homework session when my phone vibrates. Wei has sent us a writing assignment about digital media, and I'm determined to do a good job. Actually, stellar is what I'm aiming for. I'd love to be published on her website. That would be terrific for my visibility and my resumé, not to mention do wonders for my bruised ego. I heard back at last from the French design company agreeing to make me an affiliate, so I was able to publish my blog post with all those great photos, but all this stuff with Henry is making it really hard to concentrate. I look at my phone — it's Jake. It's three in the morning in New York. I text him back.

FaceTime?

Sure. Lemme jump on.
Meet you there in five.

I run to the bathroom and pour myself a glass of cold water before our chat. I just hope Jake has some good news.

I log on to FaceTime, and relief washes over me as soon as I see his face.

He's wearing his signature hipster glasses and a funny baseball cap with the words *I Don't Givenchy a Duck*. He's sipping iced coffee through a straw, so I guess all is not so bad in the world. I let out a loud sigh of relief.

"I'm so happy you reached out. I need to talk."

"Oh? What about, dearest one?"

"Henry kissed me."

"Well, I knew that was coming.... Was it good?"

"Hmm ... yes."

"Did you kiss him back?"

"Yes. It happened so quickly ..."

"You're in major trouble now, sister."

"I know. I feel really, really shitty about it. I can't believe I let it happen. I'm a bad person and I *definitely* don't deserve to have a boyfriend."

"Sometimes good things fall apart so better things can fall together," he quotes between sips of his iced coffee. "Marilyn Monroe," he adds.

He must recognize the look of panic on my face. I don't want things to fall apart.

"Listen, just play it cool, kiddo," he says. "Don't beat yourself up over it, all right?"

"I don't know what to do. Should I tell Jonathan?"

"No, I don't think so. Not right now. He's under enough stress as it is. I'm afraid you'll kill the poor guy. Wait until things get resolved in your head and in your heart."

"I feel especially weird about it after Henry's big announcement yesterday."

"What announcement?"

"He's launching a new blog about eco-fashion. It was really strange, the way it all came about."

"Is he copying you?"

"I don't think so ..."

"Whoa, Clem. This guy sounds unpredictable. Maybe that's why you're so attracted to him, he keeps you on your toes."

"Could be."

"Things will play out the way they should. Give it some time."

"Right ... What about you? Any dates?"

"Oh, a few nocturnal exchanges with a few guys, nothing worth talking about."

"And what else is happening? Are you okay?"

He looks away, then lifts his glasses and wipes away a tear. For the first time since we've logged on, I notice that his complexion is pale and drawn, as though he's lost weight, which is definitely worth worrying about.

In typical Jake fashion, he tries to put on a brave face.

"Things are rough. I'm still in the red, and those thugs keep harassing me. That's why I keep my phone shut off. They've been calling me day and night. It's a fricking nightmare. I can't sleep, Clem. All I think about is them coming over and finishing me off."

"Don't say that!"

"Um, have you seen *The Godfather*?"

"Come on, stop it."

"That's what these people do, Clem. They're evil."

I don't realize I've gone silent until Jake's voice booms through the computer. "What are you thinking, Clem? That I'm a big fat loser?"

"Stop that! You're not a loser. You're one of the most inspiring people I know, okay? Don't get down on yourself like that. And you're not fat. You've lost weight — and you need to stop that, too."

This shakes him up a bit, and he gives me a tearful smile. He doesn't do skinny — he's all about that bass. And every inch of him is what makes him so adorable.

"I just need to get out of this funk. I'm working on it. Don't give up on me, okay?"

"Never."

"So can you tell me about some more local street food? That'll help build up my appetite."

"Yes, of course. Let's see … Well, river crabs are a big part of Shanghai's food scene, but since they're only available seasonally, crab shell pies are all the rage here. They're crispy buns filled with savoury ingredients, very yummy."

"Thanks, love. I feel better already. And famished." He takes a deep breath, like he's gearing up to say something important. "So … Ellie talked to me and helped me realize I have an actual problem … She took me to one of those anonymous group meetings."

I can't believe I ever thought badly of Ellie, once upon a time. She's a heaven-sent angel.

"And?"

"It was eye-opening. It's tough to admit that you have an addiction, Clem. I feel broken." He begins to cry. My heart aches for him. Jake's one of the most authentic, big-hearted people I know. I shed tears, too, as I watch him weep.

"Listen, you're not broken, okay? The important thing is to manage it, heal, and recover. You have a brilliant fashion career ahead of you — you can't let this gambling problem get in the way of that. There's far too much at stake. These meetings will help you get better, I just know it."

He lifts his head and smiles again, wiping the tears from his cheeks. I see hope flare in his eyes. "All right, got it. Thank you, ma'am!"

"Now why don't you get back to that sewing machine, where you belong?"

"Okay, okay. I got it. I'll get cracking first thing in the morning. For you, Bonjour Girl, I'd do anything."

"Same here."

"All right, gotta go. I have a mission to accomplish."

"Love you, Jake!"

"Me, too, love. Mwah!" He puckers his lips and kisses the screen. I do the same and then sign off, my heart full of optimism.

I'm about to head back to my desk, where I'll likely be working for the rest of the afternoon and into the night, when the doorbell rings. Surprised, I look through the peephole and see a delivery man holding a towering bouquet of flowers. Oh my. I already know who they're from. My heart does somersaults. The flowers are drop-dead gorgeous. I thank the delivery man and bring them inside. I'm tempted to call Jake right back to tell him about this surprise delivery, but think better of it. He needs his sleep.

I pull out a vase from the kitchen and admire the variety: irises, roses, and white lilies. I inhale their sublime aroma. I'm flattered by Henry's thoughtful gesture. I open the little envelope that accompanies the flowers and read the note.

I hope this will help dispel any doubts you have about me …

I smell the flowers again. The truth is, I'm not sure that it does dispel my doubts. I head back to my computer and my writing project, while the delicious floral aroma still emanates from the bouquet. I have to try to forget about what happened with Henry and focus on what I was made to do. After all, if that advice is good enough for Jake, it's good enough for me, too.

Chapter Twenty-Eight

I HAVE A HUGE GRIN on my face as I reread the piece for Wei's class that I finished last night. I was up really late finishing it, then I slept through most of the morning. Unfortunately, my good feeling doesn't last long. I brew some tea, turn on my phone, and log in to WeChat.

The screen is blank except for a message: *Your account has been suspended.*

Holy *merde*.

My mouth goes dry. My eyes nearly pop out of their sockets. I can hardly breathe. My hand flies to my mouth and I knock over my cup, spilling tea onto my desk and my laptop. Has my account been shut down? I've worked so hard to build my page in China — I have tens of thousands of followers! *Merde!* What on earth is going on?

I wipe the laptop dry and use it to log in to my account. It doesn't work there, either.

I have a nauseating feeling in the pit of my stomach, an icy cold feeling that tells me something is wrong, colossally wrong. But what? Was I hacked? Did *I* do something?

I begin to pace frantically. This can't be happening. I don't know what's going on, but I know it's bad, like really bad.

I need some answers. I begin to fidget, imagining worst-case scenarios.

I follow WeChat's prescribed troubleshooting protocol to no avail, then try searching online to find out what could be happening. Maybe it's a simple glitch or a misunderstanding.

Or maybe it has to do with the fact that I'm a non-resident of this country. Something about local internet restrictions? I wish I could call Jonathan to tell him what's happening, but he's still shutting me out. Besides, the reason he won't talk to me is he thinks I'm involved with Henry ... and I can hardly deny that anymore. I'm riddled with guilt over the kiss. I want to be open, to tell Jonathan everything so we can move beyond this. But now's not the time.

I try to focus on solutions, not the problem, but I'm getting more frantic by the minute. Just when I'm about to lose it, I get a text from Jake.

What happened to your
WeChat account?

No idea! I think it was shut down

Whaaat? Just like that?

Yup. Trying not to freak out

Let me look this up and get back to
you, see what I can find out

I'm trying my best to keep it together. What have I
done wrong?

Thanks, Jake. I really
appreciate your help

My pleasure, Clem. Always
happy to help

After running various scenarios through my mind about
how to deal with the situation, I finally muster the courage
to call Henry. I need to face him like an adult.

"Hey, can we talk?"

"Sure. Is this about me kissing you or your social media
crisis?"

I let out a dry cough, and there's a long, awkward
silence. He knows about my account being shut down.
That's embarrassing.

"Um, both. We really need to chat."

"Okay, I'm all ears."

"Not over the phone. Let's meet in person."

"Where?"

"The Wild Insect Kingdom?"

"I thought you said you hated insects?"

"I had a change of heart. I'll meet you there in an hour."

Chapter Twenty-Nine

I EXIT THE SUBWAY station closest to the Wild Insect Kingdom. I walk quickly in my blue suede boots, vintage flowered dress, and pink motorcycle jacket. My hair is stacked up on top of my head in a high chignon, the style I've been wearing since I got here. I like it that way — it helps to keep my neck cool, especially when I'm feeling hot under the collar.

There are pedestrians and cars zooming everywhere. The exhaust fumes make me feel even dizzier than I was feeling already.

I wonder if anyone on the street will recognize me — *Bonjour Girl: the disgraced blogger* — and point me out. I'm no novice when it comes to facing online issues, but being in a different country without my tribe sends my insecurity skyrocketing. I just wish I had some idea what's going on.

I walk past a lovely square where a group of older people are dancing in sync to music coming from an old boombox. I stop for a moment, entranced by the beauty of this scene, where time seems to stand still. Couples are ballroom dancing in the middle of the city, looking as though they have no cares in the world. The idea of growing old with someone you love, who has your best interests at heart and wants to spend afternoons dancing in the park with you, is so romantic to me. And at the same time it's so foreign — my parents' marriage was nothing like that. But, deep down, it's what I yearn for. I just need to stop whatever it is in me that pushes love away. I've become a master at it, or so it seems. I miss Jonathan more than ever. I need to clear things up with Henry. It's the right thing to do.

I make my way inside the Wild Insect Kingdom. It looks a bit tacky, not to mention creepy. The entrance area is confusing, with giant figurines of popular cartoon characters. I'm not sure how they relate to insects, but who am I to criticize their branding strategy? Part of mine just got completely removed from the internet.

After paying the entrance fee, I look at my watch. I have a solid fifteen minutes before I meet Henry, so I decide to walk around, mostly to distract myself.

Seeing young children running about playfully puts a smile on my face. I think back to when I last felt that carefree. It feels like ages ago. Going to college makes you grow up fast. Now I understand why I wanted to come here. Being close to nature forces me to look at the bigger picture; in the grand spectrum of life and the universe and the internet, my blog is just a speck of dust. I'll survive this.

I head straight for the butterfly section. They're fascinating creatures, the way they travel and migrate and, most remarkably, transform into spectacular beauties.

I like to think that I've also undergone a massive transformation in the last year or so, from an insecure teenager to a more mature young woman with her feet on the ground. I'm proud of my accomplishments, of trying to show a different side of fashion. It's too bad my efforts are being hindered.

I move on to a different section, where bees are buzzing about. I've read that in China, the bee symbolizes vocational advancement. How ironic, given the situation I'm in. I try to look on the bright side: bees also represent sweetness, abundance, and opportunity. And in every major challenge, there's an opportunity for growth.

I walk back toward the entrance and see Henry sitting on a large rock in the far corner. He's lost in thought.

"Hi, Henry." I take a seat next to him, resting my blue suede boots on the fake moss that covers the floor.

"Hey." He looks at me and then looks down at his shoes. He seems to be at a loss for words. I feel the same way, but I find the courage to speak up first.

"Thank you for the flowers. They're gorgeous. And thanks for meeting me. I know you're really busy with school and stuff."

"I'm sorry about what happened."

"Are you talking about my WeChat account or the kiss?"

"I'm sure you're more concerned about your online presence than me kissing you."

"Both have been on my mind, actually."

"I feel like a bloody fool." He runs his fingers through his hair.

"Don't worry about the kiss, okay? I'm flattered. But it can't continue. I have a boyfriend. I love Jonathan, and I miss him. A lot."

He sighs loudly and crosses his arms. This conversation is making us both uncomfortable.

"Right. That's not exactly what I hoped to hear, but I had a feeling that's what you'd say."

"We can still be friends, can't we?"

He looks away. "I don't know …"

"Come on, Henry, we have lots in common, we like to hang out, and we've shared some pretty personal stuff."

"I know. I wish I could pretend nothing's changed, but I just don't think I can."

I can hear crickets in the background.

Henry stands up, takes my hands in his, and pulls me up off the rock. He moves in close. "Are you sure we can't try to make this work?"

I can't believe he's doing this. I really thought he'd understand. "No, Henry, don't." I push away from him.

"But —"

"No, I have to go." I turn my back on him.

"Clementine, there's something else I need to tell you —"

I feel his hand on my shoulder, but quickly slide out of his reach. "Forget it!"

As I storm off, I hear him say something about my blog, but I'm too upset to turn back. I rush out of the Wild Insect Kingdom, feeling more like a squished bug than a butterfly.

On my way home, I come across a street vendor selling giant teddy bears. These are all over the city; vendors wheel around racks of almost life-sized bears, and you can buy them pretty much anytime and anywhere, including in the middle of the night, in bars and in nightclubs. Nothing oozes love like a bear nearly as big as you are.

I consider buying one. It would temporarily fill the void in my heart and bring me the comfort I crave. But I decide against it. My down comforter and flannel PJs will do for now.

Chapter Thirty

IT'S NEARLY DARK when I arrive at Sandra's apartment. After leaving the Wild Insect Kingdom, I went for a long walk to get some perspective. At first, being close to nature and animals soothed me, but now it's brought out a primal part of me instead. I went back to my apartment and tried to work for a few hours, but I just couldn't. I finally called Sandra, and she invited me over.

I generally try not to bite my nails, but times of crisis like these bring out my worst habits. As I chew on the blue sparkles at the tips of my fingers, I think of my WeChat account and all the months I spent building it, picture by picture, post by post — and I feel furious. I start in on the other hand as I chew over how badly things went with Henry. I can't deal with any more tension right now, I just can't.

I am so glad Sandra invited me over. I just know she's the right person to talk to. Thank god she responded to my SOS.

Her high-rise building, located in the Jing'an neighbourhood, is very swanky. The doorman calls up to announce my arrival, then waves me in. He's grinning and nodding and making friendly gestures as though I'm family. I'm not sure what she said to him over the intercom — maybe something like what she said on the plane, that I was like a daughter to her? The thought of it warms my heart.

I ride up the tall windowed elevators, and my breath nearly stops when I catch the spectacular views of the city below. The sea of bright lights, the majestic river, and the futuristic cityscape are almost surreal. The scenery lifts my mood as the elevator takes me higher and higher.

I just need to find the strength to face my challenges head on.

I knock on Sandra's door and hear footsteps. I already start to relax, reassured that someone mature, loving, and kind is coming to my rescue.

"Hello, dear Clementine! Please, come in. I've made some tea." Sandra looks comfortable in a blue V-neck sweater, lounge pants, and beige slippers. "Let me get your coat."

I hand over my motorcycle jacket and she looks at it with a glint in her eye. I wonder if she would have worn something like it in her younger days.

I follow her down the narrow hallway decorated with antique rugs and blue and white vases holding branches covered in blooming cherry blossoms. We pass a room filled with contemporary art and the sweet smell of jasmine. There are books everywhere: paperbacks, rare editions, and coffee table books on art, design, and home decor. Her collection makes me drool.

"All right, I'm ready to move in!" I say, joking to try to lighten my troubled mood.

Sandra laughs and gives me a curious look. She probably thinks she'd like the company. But not in the state I'm in, she wouldn't.

We make our way to a sitting area where a silver tea set is waiting. A painting on the far wall catches my eye. It's a portrait of Sandra when she was younger. In it, she's very attractive with her red lips and dreamy eyes.

"Wow, you look beautiful."

"Thank you. My father had it commissioned after I graduated from college. He was so proud."

This gives me goosebumps. I look at her with much admiration. Sandra is grand. Sandra is solid. Sandra is wise, and she's supremely romantic. I want to be like her when I grow up. But more importantly, Sandra gives me hope, something I need right now.

"And your apartment is stunning. It could be a set for a film."

"Horror or romance?" she shoots back wryly.

"Romance, of course!" We both laugh at that.

"Thank you. I had an apartment in Hong Kong, but I sold it and bought this place when I decided to live here part-time, so I could be closer to my brother and his kids. And now to my sister, who's in the hospital. It does the trick nicely."

"Yes, I'd say so," I say, admiring the beautiful paintings on the walls. "It must make you so happy to look at these."

"Yes, very happy. This is where I spend my mornings. I like to read, reflect, and gaze at the art."

"Reflection is a good thing. I could use some of that right now," I say, staring into my cup of tea.

She pats me on the shoulder gently. "You're in the right place. I call this my reflecting room."

She offers me some cookies on a plate, but I shake my head. "No, thank you. I've kind of lost my appetite after today."

"Oh? Something about the young man who was waiting for you at the airport?"

"Henry. Well, yes and no. He kissed me the other night, and I feel terrible about that."

She takes a long sip of tea, leaving a trace of lipstick on her cup. "Is that so bad?"

"I have a boyfriend in New York, remember? Jonathan."

"And who is it that truly makes your heart sing?"

"Jonathan. I miss him so much. It was a terrible mistake," I admit, holding back tears.

"Okay, well, now you know. Focus on the future, not what's behind you. Consider it a learning experience."

"You're right. I just wish he were here so I could tell him how I feel. He's been avoiding my calls, and I feel terrible."

"Don't worry, Clementine. It'll blow over, for sure. You never told me much about Jonathan. What is it about him that you miss the most?"

"Lots of things: his kindness, his loving presence, his comforting touch, his unconditional support. I also miss his creativity. He's a very talented photographer."

"What kind of photography?"

"Portraits, fashion, some corporate work, too."

"I've been asked to help promote a local exhibit on international photography. I'd love to see the type of work that he does. Can you send me some links to his work?

Maybe I could get one of his pieces in there at the last minute."

"Oh, Sandra, that would be amazing. Thank you! I'll send you his media kit. I'm sure he'll be very grateful."

"Now why are you still looking so sad?"

"There's something else going on. My WeChat account has been suspended."

"Oh dear. Does this have a big impact on you?"

"As a blogger, pretty major." I feel tears coming up. "And I'm still in the dark as to why it happened."

Sandra squeezes my hand like the caring friend I need right now. "Is there any way to fix it?"

"I'm not sure. I don't really know what else to do …"

"Here, sweetie, let me get you a tissue." Sandra goes out, and by the time she comes back with a tissue box, I'm a blubbering mess.

"I feel really comfortable talking to you, Sandra. I guess that's why I'm here." I blow my nose in a tissue — not the most elegant gesture, but hey, it's the medicine I need. "I told you that you're like the mother I wish I had … That's because my mom has been involved in some un-motherly behaviour in the past." I blow my nose again.

"That does happen."

"Yes, it does, but with her, it happened a lot. How often does a typical mother make out with her daughter's boyfriend while her daughter is in the next room?" I blurt out angrily. It just had to come out. At this point, I don't care — I need to vent. "But that's just the tip of the iceberg. She made me promise never to tell my dad, making me an accomplice to her behaviour. And I agreed, just to protect him," I say, as tears run down my cheeks.

Sandra looks away with a pained expression, as though this is too much to take in. "Oh, Clementine, I'm so sorry. What an awful thing to go through." She opens her arms and I nestle my head against her chest and sob. Total waterworks. And although I must sound awful, it feels good.

"I know someone who could help you deal with your painful past. Help you heal, open your heart, and make the right decisions."

"Who?"

She smiles, with a twinkle in her eyes. "A Chinese herbalist."

I envision myself sitting in an old Chinese apothecary, surrounded by mysterious ingredients and potions. It gives me goosebumps.

"Do you believe in the power of healing therapies like herbs, Clementine?"

"Sure," I say half-heartedly. I have always wanted to believe in stuff like that. I'm willing to try anything.

"Why don't you stay over tonight, and we can see him tomorrow. How does that sound?"

"It sounds great," I say with a smile. "Thank you so much for being here for me. It means the world." I blow my nose one last time and decide to try a cookie. It may not be as powerful as ancient Chinese herbs, but it'll lift my mood. That'll have to do for now.

Chapter Thirty-One

I ONCE READ a magazine interview with a professional athlete who said that every morning, his dad had him look in the mirror and repeat, "Today is going to be a great day. I can, and I will."

Reading this made me jealous; I wished my dad had done something like that for me. Now, whenever I'm feeling anxious or insecure, no matter what's going on, I repeat those same words to myself.

I wake up in the morning, comfortably ensconced in an uber comfortable bed with high-thread-count sheets and designer pillows, surrounded by books, artwork, and fresh flowers, and wearing pyjamas by Olivia von Halle, who apparently once lived in Shanghai. They're made of the softest silk, with navy and cream stripes, and were apparently inspired by the pyjamas Coco Chanel wore. Like those slightly eccentric pyjama-wearing Shanghai locals, I'd have no problem prancing around town in these sumptuous creations. They make me feel like one of those glamorous Hollywood starlets with a big online following … except that I've completely lost mine in Asia, and my life is in shambles.

But I try to forget about it for now. Sandra's here to support me, and soon some herbalist's potions will dissolve all my troubles. At least that's what I tell myself.

I see my cell looming on the dresser next to Sandra's beautiful bottles of French perfume. There's also a framed photo of a younger Sandra standing in front of a train with a dashing Asian man behind her. He's looking away from the camera, but holding her by the waist. Sandra has clearly had more than one big romance, which is not surprising given how warm and magnetic she is.

I pick up my phone. Maybe losing my WeChat account is the best thing that could have happened. I can just call it a day, begin again with a new concept, new title, and new life. Maybe the lesson is that my self-esteem shouldn't be attached to the number of followers I have, because they can all be taken away in a heartbeat.

I think of Jonathan. I miss his sweet texts and his unshakable support. As I turn on my phone, I'm hoping that I'll finally have a message from the man I love … and I do.

As soon as the phone powers up, messages flood in from Jonathan, Jake, Maddie, and Henry. My heart is beating fast as I open the first text:

> Hi there,
>
> Sorry for being so lame and not writing sooner.
>
> I've been in meetings with some pretty difficult people. Lawyers and

businessmen who want to tear me
down. All this fighting and confrontation
is zapping my energy.

I miss you. I miss us. But we both
need to focus on our priorities right
now. Jake told me about your WeChat
situation. I know how hard you've been
working at it. You're a star, Clem, and
it sounds like somebody or something
wants to take you down. Don't let them.
Okay?

It will work out for each of us, and for
us.

Stay strong. Let the storm blow over.

I'll see you on the other side.

J. XO

What a relief to finally hear from him! His message
may be a bit distant, but I'll take this over the silent treatment any day. I'm just happy that he still cares. I can't wait
to go back to the way things were. And I'm optimistic that
we'll get there.

I read Jake's message next:

I tried contacting WeChat. No luck,
sorry. You can't let them shut down your
account! No, no, no! You need to appeal
this and fight for your rights. Do not let
this affect your online reputation, okay?
You've invested way too much time in
this! You need to deal with it now!

Jake always makes me smile. He really is supportive of all that I do. What would I ever do without him?

Maddie's message provides still more support:

> Clementine! Jake sent me an email
> about your WeChat account. So sorry
> to hear about that. Call me when you
> have a sec, okay? I'm worried about
> you! XOXO

There's a string of texts from Henry that leaves me feeling torn and perplexed:

> I'd like to talk to you again. I hope you
> can forgive me.

> Whatever you do, please don't shut me
> out, I'm so sorry about everything. You
> mean a lot to me.

> I tried calling last night. Please don't
> give me the silent treatment.

> There's something important I need to
> tell you.

I'm not sure what to do about Henry. Should I talk to him? I'm not sure I want to. At least not yet. I need to let things blow over a bit before I can face him again ...

I think about Sandra, her warm hospitality, her kindness, and I decide to put on a brave face for her sake and mine. I type up a short post for my blog telling my readers that my WeChat account was deactivated, and I'm investigating the matter. I assure them that I'll be back soon.

Today is a great day. I can, and I will ...

Chapter Thirty-Two

"SLEEP WELL, I PRESUME?" Sandra asks as I walk out onto the balcony. She's also wearing silk pyjamas, hers covered in large blue and white blooms, and is stretched out along the railing with tea and a newspaper, enjoying the spectacular view. She looks regal and confident, as if the city below is hers for the taking. Based on that article I read about her in *Vogue China*, it is. I'm so grateful to have met her. But for some reason, she doesn't look as cheerful as she did last night.

"These pyjamas are sumptuous. I feel like a queen wearing them."

"That is exactly what you are, and frankly, it's time you started acting like one."

Whoa. I take a step back and lean against the door. This is a much more direct side to Sandra. I guess years of working in high finance will teach you to be that way.

She sees my surprised reaction and her face softens.

"Sorry," she says, looking into the distance. "My sister's illness has taken a turn for the worse, and it's getting to me. I spoke to her doctor this morning, and it sounds like her disease has progressed." I can see tears in the corners of her eyes. "She has young children — it's not easy, you know?"

"There's no need to apologize, Sandra. I'm so sorry to hear that." I place a hand on her shoulder. She pats it tenderly.

"Thank you. I'm glad you stayed last night. I needed the company just as much as you did. Have you had any ideas about how to handle your WeChat problem yet?"

She gets up and makes her way to the kitchen. I follow and watch her brew some more jasmine tea.

"That's what Jake and Jonathan texted me about this morning, among other things."

She gives me a puzzled look, then shakes her head. "Your mind is consumed with men and what *they* think about things. It should be the other way around, okay?" She points her teaspoon at me. "That shouldn't be your preoccupation right now, Clementine. Men come and go, but your name — well, that stays with you forever. You need to protect it with your life."

"How can I when I don't even know why this is happening?"

"You must, and you will!"

I take a deep breath. "You're right. I need to do something. I'll get in touch with the WeChat customer service department, and as soon as I get home, I'll post more about it on my blog."

"Good. That's what I like to hear."

"So are we still seeing this herbalist today? I sure could use something to help me cope with this mess."

She smiles. "Absolutely. He's expecting us at his office at ten thirty. We'll leave as soon as you're ready."

"Perfect. Thank you, Sandra, for everything. I mean it."

We clink our teacups together, just like Maddie and I do.

Dr. Ho's office is on a tiny side street in Nanshi, the old Chinese city, near the Old Town Bazaar, Yu Garden, the Old City Wall, and the Confucian Temple. According to Sandra, Dr. Ho is kind, knowledgeable, and big-hearted. I'll try to remain open-minded, though I'm skeptical. What could a traditional herbalist possibly prescribe to alleviate the sadness caused by a suspended social media account?

After walking up several flights of stairs, we arrive out of breath in his small, nondescript office space. Piled high on shelves against the white walls are stacks and stacks of dried medicinal herbs in tiny bags and jars.

Unlike the high-end shops, cafés, and bars I've frequented in the city, this office feels like it belongs somewhere back in time. It's actually a refreshing change from the ultra-modern, sleek metropolis.

There's a large black-and-white poster at the front entrance with an inscription in Mandarin: *The secrets to vibrant health: Do not smoke, drink, or be pessimistic.*

I smile and tell myself that two out of three isn't bad. Or is it one out of three? I have been drinking a bit lately, and my mood is in the dumps. I wonder if the doctor will be able to tell.

Sandra nods for me to take a seat. She's wearing a colourful silk wrap dress that's flattering to her figure. My guess is that she's wearing these bold, happy colours to hide her sadness, something I sometimes do myself.

Next to Sandra, my outfit looks tired; I'm wearing the same clothes as yesterday. But I doubt Dr. Ho will care. Looking around his office, I'd guess he isn't the type to be too concerned with such frivolities.

Before we left her apartment, I did spray on some of Sandra's Armani Privé Pivoine Suzhou. According to Sandra, the scent was inspired by the traditional gardens of Suzhou, a city considered to be China's Venice of the East. I hope to have enough free time and peace of mind at some point to visit it.

After a few minutes, I hear my name called out from a room down the hall. Sandra nods for me to go. "Go ahead, you'll see that he's lovely. I know he can help you. My family has been going to him for years."

"All right, if you say so."

I walk into the tiny room and am surprised to discover that Dr. Ho is nothing like what I was expecting. He's got a white goatee, and perched on his head is a wool hat like one of those toques worn by rappers. He's wearing a denim shirt, old khaki pants, and a beige lab coat that looks as old as his practice must be. The look is mad professor meets cool downtown dude, except that this cool dude is at least ninety-three years old.

"Please, take a seat here," he instructs me in heavily accented English.

I sit on his examination table and he asks me to stick out my tongue. No *hello, nice to meet you*, no pleasantries at all. He gets right down to business. I guess the kindness comes later.

"Your perfume is no good. Too strong for your skin. No more of that."

I guess Dr. Ho is not a fan of Armani.

"Wear only natural, essential oils. They're much better for you."

"Thanks for the advice," I say, cringing at the thought of getting rid of all the French perfumes my parents have given me on my birthdays over the years.

I hold my tongue out while he studies it attentively. I can see that behind his intense gaze are the eyes of a kind soul. He's dedicated his life to helping people feel better, and it shows. He could light up half the city with his warm glow.

"You drink coffee?"

"Um, yes, I do." I can't lie about that. It's written all over my face and tongue, apparently.

"You drink too much of it. Stop that. It's bad for your liver," he says.

I nod with clenched teeth. How am I going to survive school and everything else in my life without coffee? I guess there could be worse things, like if he asked me to cut back on the *pain au chocolat* I get from the bakery down the street every morning.

"And too much sugar. Polluting your system. You need to stop that, too."

Ha, there it is. I'm starting to regret coming here. What else is he going to tell me? To stop shopping for clothes?

He then begins to rub my back vigorously. It feels good at first, but quickly becomes painful. I want to tell him to stop, but imagine it would be futile.

"Much stress inside of you," he says while he rubs. It feels as though my skin might peel off.

"Yes, a whole lot of stress," I tell him. "Boyfriend trouble, plus my WeChat account was suspended. Can you believe it?"

He stops what he's doing and comes back around to the front of the table. "We what?"

I guess that's another secret to vibrant health that's missing from his poster: *Don't spend all your time on social media; it can suck the life out of you.*

I shake my head. "Never mind. It's not important."

He grins. "Just kidding! I know about internet stuff! Young people are too concerned about that! Too much technology and spending all the time looking at your phone. It's no good for your neck, no good for your shoulders, and no good for your spirit."

"You got that right," I murmur under my breath.

"And no good for your heart, either," he says, pressing his hand into the middle of my chest. "You need to release all this sadness here."

"How do I do that?"

"Just close your eyes. Let it go," he says as he continues to press hard. Within seconds, tears begin to run down my cheeks.

"Okay, good. Now, just let it out. This is important for your life force and self-esteem."

I sit there crying as he presses on my chest.

"You are a very strong girl. So much stronger than you think."

"Thank you," I say, sniffling. "I'm glad I came here. I was feeling defeated."

"No, never give up! Look at me, I'm old! And I don't use technology!"

I sigh. "I know."

"Internet creates too much temptation. Too many choices. It confuses your head. Makes you want things you don't need. And all that online shopping, that's no good for your energy, either. You are leaking energy through your eyes by staring at and wanting all that stuff! You must stop wanting all these things you don't need!"

"I know you're right, but ... how can I be successful as a fashion blogger without shopping for clothes or using social media?"

He shakes his head, not swayed by my argument. "I'm talking about your health, physical and mental. Are you listening? My parents had no money. I had to search for food in the fields just to eat, but that's why I'm still alive today. Just vegetables. No meat and no technology. Just simple living. That's why I'm happy." He grins.

"Okay, fine. What about my boy trouble? Do you have anything to help me with that?"

He stops pressing on my chest, stares me in the eye, and just cackles. I don't see what's so funny. There's nothing funny about any of this.

"I'm sad," I explain. "I miss my boyfriend back home. I acted poorly and he's upset with me and I feel terrible. That's what's stuck in my chest."

"Pfft, boyfriends. Don't worry about them! What's important is the health of your spirit and your soul!" He holds each of my eyelids wide open and examines my eyes. "Stop focusing so much on men. That's just nonsense. True love cannot be chased, and it never dies. It comes to you when you find balance within yourself: the yin and the yang."

"Well, I can tell I'm a bit out of balance."

"A bit?"

"Okay, probably a lot. And what about my family?"

"What about it?"

"I visited some relatives in Shanghai recently, and I don't think they approve of my career. They think I should be a lawyer or a doctor. I didn't think their opinion really mattered at first, but it's starting to have a negative effect on me."

Dr. Ho just stares at me and begins to laugh again.

"Who cares about what family thinks? Are they all super, super happy?"

"They look okay, maybe not super, super happy."

"Why do you listen to them, then? They're just projecting their unhappiness and fears on you. Ignore it! Just follow your heart, okay? You will thrive!"

"All right. If you say so."

"I'll give you some herbs to help with all of this."

"That would be much appreciated. Thank you."

"And I must tell you something. There's someone around you that's no good. Bad energy. Watch out, okay?"

Oh no. I have enough bad vibes already. Who's he talking about? "Man or woman?" I ask.

"I don't know. I just feel the energy of deception!" His voice is so loud as he says this that I nearly fall off the examination table. He sure has a tough love approach to advice. He could make a fortune on YouTube.

I get off the table, thank him profusely for his suggestions, and head for the waiting area to find Sandra. After we pay for the consultation and the herbs, I want to get out of here as fast as I can. Assuming the doctor is right, I need to root out whoever's deceiving me, because the last thing I need in my life right now is more chaos.

I need to cut it off before it begins.

Again.

Chapter Thirty-Three

ACCORDING TO CONFUCIUS, another wise dude, "silence is a true friend who never betrays."

That's what I'm thinking as Sandra and I ride back from Dr. Ho's office. I haven't said anything since we left. I'm processing everything that he said to me.

His words of wisdom resonated powerfully with me, especially the part about technology and social media leaving a gaping hole in my heart. I was bullied on Twitter by Stella, seduced on Instagram by Henry, and now I've had my WeChat account suspended. What will happen next? He's probably right — it's all a waste of time and energy.

Other thoughts swim through my mind like the koi in the pond at Yu Garden. Why am I such a magnet for this stuff? What have I ever done to deserve any of this? Why can't I just find peace and enjoy a carefree, creative life?

I take a deep breath and try to be calm. According to Dr. Ho, pessimism leads to ill health. I need to watch the negative thinking.

"Do you want to talk about anything that he said?" Sandra asks. "You don't have to — it's up to you." She pats me softly on the knee.

"He said a lot of things," I say, staring out the window. I don't mention what Dr. Ho said about perfume. I don't want to hurt her feelings. "He said I drink too much coffee and eat too much sugar."

She giggles. "He said that to me, too."

"Did he tell you to stop shopping online?" I ask.

She laughs. "He didn't have to. I'm not a big shopper. I have to force myself into the stores whenever I have to buy a dress for one of those galas I get invited to. It's just not my cup of tea."

"You can afford clothes from the fanciest stores and talented designers, but you don't like to shop? You're something else, Sandra," I say, amazed. I could learn a lot from her.

"I prefer to invest in art, rare books, and promising young people like you. But that's just me. There's nothing wrong with loving clothes, Clementine. Fashion is your passion, not mine. You have so much fun with it, too. I mean, look at you — you're like a walking piece of art. You take it to another level."

"Thanks, Sandra. That means a lot."

"But, while you may be wearing fun clothes, you still look a bit down and out. Did the doctor say anything that was helpful to you?"

"He said to focus on happiness and balance within, and not worry about men. I think he's on to something."

Our conversation is interrupted by the ringing of her cellphone from inside her handbag. She glances at it, then back at me with a look of barely concealed panic.

"You can answer, I don't mind."

"It's okay. I'll call them back later. It can wait."

I can't help feeling that she's hiding something. But what?

I don't tell her that Dr. Ho hinted at some kind of deception in my life. I have a feeling that whatever it is, the betrayal has already happened. But she probably senses from my silence that I'm worried about something.

"No matter what happens," she says, "just remember: you're much stronger than you think."

I smile broadly. That's exactly what Dr. Ho said. Great minds think alike.

Now, if I could only convince myself of it, too.

As soon as I'm back in my apartment, I text Jake.

Are you there?

Yup! Calling …

His face appears on my screen in FaceTime. "At your service, babe, rain or shine, night or day, rich or poor. Mostly the latter at the moment, but that's beside the point. So, did you appeal?"

"No, just got back from the doctor."

"What? Why? Are you sick?"

"Sick, no. Heartbroken and confused, yes."

"I'm sorry. So what did the doctor say?"

"You don't want to know."

"Of course I want to know! Come on, Clemy."

"He gave me some herbs."

"To smoke?"

"No, to drink in a tea."

"Oh."

"And he said to cut out sugar, coffee, shopping, perfume, and chasing men."

"That sucks. Anything else?"

"He said something weird. I'm not sure what to make of it."

"What?"

"Apparently some kind of deception is hovering around me ..."

"No kidding. Again?"

"Maybe he was just sensing the Stella incident."

"Yeah, probably. Her vibes are so toxic, you could probably sense them from the next galaxy."

"Do you think she could be behind what happened to my WeChat?"

"Could be. The girl is wicked, Clem. I don't trust her, no matter how many legal documents Parsons made her sign before she left."

"We'll find out. We always do," I say, though I'm feeling deflated.

"Come on, Clem, be a warrior. Don't give up!"

"I'm trying. Thank god you're in my life. I'd be lost without you. Is everything okay on your end?"

"Ellie's still helping me out, and the first batch of skirts is nearly done. The two of you really are saving my ass. Otherwise, I'd be up shit creek in a body bag."

"And the twelve-step program?"

He sighs. "It has its ups and downs. But I'm committed and I found a sponsor."

"That's great, Jake. I'm so proud of you."

"Yeah, yeah. So what are you going to do next? Work on the online situation, I hope?"

"I'll get to work on that, on one condition."

"Shoot."

"That you get back to your sewing machine at the same time. I want to see results! Including some new pieces for that great idea about clothes for people with arthritis."

"Done. Love ya."

"Me, too. Times a million."

"Awwwwww."

Chapter Thirty-Four

I FURIOUSLY TYPE up an email to WeChat's customer service asking for guidance on how to retrieve my account. Finally, someone responds to ask for more information, so I write back, explaining that my account was suspended without warning or explanation. I'm hoping for some sympathy here, considering months of hard work are at stake.

While I wait for a reply, armed with Sandra's advice, a good night's sleep, and Dr. Ho's herbs, I try to come up with something intelligent to write for my blog, but just blank out. I decide to go for a walk instead.

I head to Fuzhou Road, the avenue with all the bookshops that I read about in *Vogue China*. Maybe I'll find a book about how to handle social media disasters.

I exit the subway in front of Shanghai Book City, the largest bookstore in town, a literary shrine that reminds me of some of my favourite bookstores in New York City. At the front of the store, popular English titles like the Harry Potter series are displayed. I'm curious to know how many locals actually read these titles.

I stop a young sales clerk with cool hipster glasses and speak to him in Mandarin. "Hi, I was wondering, are these books popular with locals?"

"No, not really, they're more for you tourists," he answers in English.

How does he know I'm a tourist? Is it the way I speak or dress? Should I be offended? I don't know what to think anymore.

"So what *is* popular? What do you recommend?"

"Young people don't read paper books that much anymore. They mostly read stuff online: short stories, blogs, social media posts."

"I see." As a book lover, that's sad to hear.

"But they do seem to like these types of fantasy books," the sales clerk continues, pointing to some large stacks of martial arts novels. The cover art looks like something out of an action-themed video game, and the authors apparently use pen names like "Eagle in the Dust" and "Addicted to Your Pale Cheek."

I pick one up. I could give it to Jake as a souvenir. I bet he'd get a kick out of it. I'm flipping through the pages when I hear a vaguely familiar male voice. I freeze. Who is that? A fellow student? I close my eyes and then it hits me: it's Henry's friend and website partner, Stephen.

He's talking to someone in an aisle nearby.

In no mood to talk to him, I start to discreetly make my way toward the exit. But then curiosity gets the better of me. I duck behind a book display and peer around it.

Stephen is leaning against a bookcase, talking to a woman I know. It's Masha, the karaoke queen. They're giggling and whispering, and then he kisses her. So I guess the two of them are dating. That's not so surprising; from what Henry has told me they both love fashion, selfies, and the spotlight. I'm about to tiptoe away when I overhear something that pulls me up short.

"Pretty sure she still has no clue what happened to her account," Stephen murmurs. "But she's about to find out in a big way!"

Masha giggles in response.

I stand there, feet frozen on the grey-tiled floor. They're talking about me. My mind spins furiously in search of an explanation. What the hell is going on?

The answer arrives in the form of a buzzing on my phone — an email from the WeChat customer service team.

Hello, Ms. Liu,

Your account was shut down after we received a complaint from an account called Eco-Couture. It claims you violated our terms of conduct by profiling a piece of gifted merchandise without full disclosure. Also, it was alleged that your most recent post was offensive. You may appeal this decision by taking the following steps ...

There it is, in all its glory. What Dr. Ho predicted and what my intuition failed to detect yet again. Major deception.

I can't believe it. Who knew people could wear such false masks so convincingly? Well, okay, I guess I did — or should have. Another lesson I've learned: all that shines on the internet isn't gold. As a matter of fact, it can be as dark as a piece of coal.

Was Henry in on this crap all along? Was his over-the-top charm offensive all an act? Was he scheming with Stephen since before I even arrived here? The fact that my relationship with Jonathan was jeopardized because of this fake-ass guy makes me want to vomit on the bestsellers.

I'm right in the middle of another Tower moment, as they call it in tarot card readings — a moment when you fail to pay attention to the signs and go against your better judgment. I'm on a roll these days.

I drop the paperback on a random shelf and run out onto the street, looking for some way to regain my sense of self-respect. At this point, that may be hard to do.

Chapter Thirty-Five

BACK AT MY APARTMENT, I'm feeling completely dejected. I didn't listen to my inner voice, and now I'm paying for it. As soon as Henry and Stephen announced their new website, I should've known they were up to no good. More than anything, I feel like a fool. I almost lost Jonathan over what was, apparently, a stupid, *fake* flirtation.

I go straight to my laptop and discover tons of negative comments on my last blog post about the local fashion scene. I long ago turned off phone notifications for blog comments, so I can make sure I'm in a proper frame of mind before reading them. I'm actually glad that I didn't see these negative comments sooner. And "negative" doesn't really do justice to some of these comments. "Brutal" would be more accurate. Words like "insulting," "offensive," "traitor," and even "racist" jump out at me.

My heart pounds in my chest. For a split second, I wonder if this is some kind of revenge plot orchestrated by Stella, my bully from last year. But it isn't. One of the commenters shares a link to a website called *Bloggers Unveiled*.

Their mission statement: "To enlighten the public on the deceptive activities of the world's most prolific influencers." The short article says,

> At a time when anxiety and depression are at a high, you would think these bloggers would know better than to engage in shady practices! But some of them do not! In her most recent post, Clementine Liu shares photos of herself wearing a comped shirt without acknowledging that she received it in exchange for her coverage. She also shares affiliate links to the Victoire & Sophie website. Her collaboration with the offensive designer is demeaning to the people of Shanghai, where she's currently studying in an exchange program at a posh fashion school.

Comped shirt? They must mean the blouse from Henry … but it was a gift! I don't get it.

And worse, an offensive designer? Demeaning to the residents of Shanghai? My post mentioned that Victoire & Sophie were investing millions into an upcoming local runway event. How could that be construed as offensive?

A quick online search turns up the answer. My face falls as the headlines pop up. There are multiple articles from prominent international news sites, all dated less than forty-eight hours ago.

Victoire & Sophie's Shanghai runway show has been cancelled after head
designer Olivier Leroux made disrespect-
ful comments to a popular blogger about
Shanghai designers, calling them "a bunch
of backward dilettantes with little taste or
talent."

Oh merde. I feel faint, and my stomach clenches.
I missed all this while I was holed up at Sandra's. I'm
usually so on top of these things. I can't believe this is
happening. I quickly delete the offending post and drop
my face into my hands. I feel terrible, bruised and raw.
Being attacked like this again is bringing back such painful memories, but unlike last semester, I'm all alone. I
don't have Maddie, Jonathan, or Jake here to support me.
I'm so far away from them.

Even though those angry comments have now been
deleted along with the post, one of them is burned into my
memory: "How could you, Clementine Liu? You say you
promote ethics in fashion and YOU'RE acting unethically!
AND COLLABORATING WITH RACISTS!"

I can barely suppress my tears. I've been pouring my
heart and soul into this blog. How could anyone question
my ethics? My integrity? What will the faculty of Condé
Nast think of me now?

All the anxiety I felt after Stella's attacks comes flowing
right back. I feel like I'm being stabbed in the chest.

I failed to pay attention to my intuition big time. I
should have listened to my inner voice when I had doubts
about doing business with Victoire & Sophie.

I'm reminded of that old saying, *Fool me once, shame on you; fool me twice, shame on me.* How could I have been so careless?

Thankfully, Jake appears online, not a moment too soon. I phone him immediately.

"Thank god you're still up. Some pretty nasty stuff has been going on."

"I know. Whatever you do, Clem, don't panic, okay? You've been down this road before. You're a champ."

"It's so awful! People think I intentionally collaborated with a racist? What will the school think? And my dad's family? What will my cousins and Aunt Jiao think? Will anyone believe this was a colossal misunderstanding?"

I undo the topknot in my hair, kick off my sneakers, and lie down on the living room floor. I try to breathe deeply and relax as Jake's voice floats out of my phone.

"I do believe you, but I don't know about the readers. I'm sorry to say this, honey, but the noise has reached a fever pitch. There are over five thousand retweets of that *Bloggers Unveiled* article denouncing you as an irresponsible ..."

Holy crap. I fling an arm over my eyes, trying to get my bearings, but it doesn't work. My mind spins. What will everyone at *Parsons* think? And my dad? He'll be devasted by all this negative attention. I want the floor to swallow me whole.

I'm suddenly filled with rage. Why was I following someone else's vision for my blog instead of my own, anyway? The only reason I tried the affiliated link was because Brian pushed me to be more commercial. So much for thinking outside the box — now I've been placed in one.

"What is Twitter saying about me, exactly?"

"A few things ... That blouse you're wearing in the photo — was it a gift from the store?"

"No, Henry bought it for me."

"Just a *friend*, huh?"

"This isn't the time, Jake."

"Sorry. Are you sure it was from him? 'Cause this *Bloggers Unveiled* page did some research, and it looks like it was gifted by the store ... and that's the problem, kiddo. You didn't disclose in your write-up the fact that you received free merch."

"Henry told me he was buying it for me."

"Maybe he wasn't telling you the whole truth?"

"Obviously. I swear I had no idea it was a freebie ... damn it." I never should have accepted that blouse. Even then, I knew something wasn't right. I could never have predicted this particular course of events, but I still should've listened to myself.

Jake continues. "And then there's the issue of the Victoire & Sophie ..."

"I obviously had no clue the designer was such an A-hole! God, how awful! I need to go deal with this fallout."

"I wish I could be there to help, Clem."

"You are helping. Now wish me luck."

"You don't need luck — you're a pro."

I finish the call, then slip into my PJs and try to figure out how to deal with this mess. I could report Henry to the Condé Nast program director for unethical behaviour, but that just feels childish.

I could have Jake and Ellie start an online smear campaign against Henry and Stephen to give them a taste of their own medicine — but again, I'm not going there. It would only create more chaos.

I could publicly accuse Henry of stealing my blog concept and scheming to get my WeChat account shut down, but then I'd only be replicating what all those trolls are doing to me now. As Maddie would say, two wrongs don't make a right.

As I sip on Dr. Ho's herbal concoction, it dawns on me that most of the world's most talented artists share an important quality: vulnerability. A sense of vulnerability is what connects you to others, doubly so in the case of artists like writers and bloggers — it creates an important connection to your audience.

I'll roll up my sleeves and simply share my truth. I will put down my weapons and reveal no names.

I don't know why I'm so nervous. I take a deep breath and let the inspiration flow.

> Dear readers,
> The recent firestorm surrounding posts on this blog and to my social media accounts has brought nothing but negative publicity and pain, so I've decided to set the record straight.
>
> It's been heartbreaking to be the target of accusations that are hurtful and, more importantly, untrue.
>
> I've been portrayed as unethical, a racist, a traitor, and a fraud. I am none of those things. BUT despite that fact, I'm taking full responsibility for what is being said about me. Yes, that's right: total, complete responsibility.

All of it is my own doing — or undoing — ALL of it.

Why? Because I didn't listen to my INNER VOICE, which has gotten me through thick and thin in the past. In the effort to pump up my own sense of self-esteem and the influence of this blog, I ignored my inner voice. And as a result, I connected myself with people who would end up bringing me down.

At the Song Liung boutique, I was offered a Liu Min blouse. My belief was that the blouse had been bought for me by a friend who was present. In fact, it was gifted to me by the store, unbeknownst to me — however, I should have asked more questions, and ultimately, I should have avoided writing about the blouse altogether, according to my editorial standards.

Since the launch of my blog, I have refused paid endorsements, as I wish to maintain my creative freedom at all costs. But I recently went against those principles and accepted compensation from a designer in exchange for publicity. This was a huge mistake. I compromised my own standards, and I did not do nearly enough to vet the standards of the designer I was affiliating myself with, something I regret immensely. I certainly did not intend to offend anyone, especially not the people of Shanghai, one of the world's greatest cities.

And still I have gone even further down a deep black hole of misery; all of this nonsense has nearly caused me to lose the most precious relationship I have with a person that I love. I treated him poorly, and he didn't deserve that.

If I could share one piece of advice, it would be this: whatever you do, dear readers and friends, never put your self-respect, friendship, or love on the line in exchange for more likes and follows, or the lure of fame and material success, because I can promise you that in the end, it's not worth it. It's all an illusion. And it can be taken away from you in an instant — *poof!*

As an esteemed teacher of mine said recently, the bubble of social media influence will burst one day —it's just a question of when. So I ask you, what is truly important? The answer is you: your instincts, your heart, your talent, and your strength. None of that can ever be taken from you. Ever. That is, unless you choose to give it away …

I could place the blame on a deceptive person who I'd thought was a friend, but turned out not to be. I could blame a teacher for encouraging me to veer off course, or my own family and my complicated childhood. I could blame social media for becoming a breeding ground for mean-spirited trolls. But the fact of the matter is that I created my own reality. Overconfidence made me think I deserved to be paid for advertising a designer's content, regardless of who the designer was. I have learned my lesson. This was a colossal error on my part.

Thanks to the help of a very wise man and a kind new friend, I've discovered that what happens to us is often a direct reflection of how we feel inside. I have been conflicted about my blog and its editorial direction, and conflict is what I attracted — lots of it — as well as an individual who didn't have my best interests at heart. Why? Because I didn't have my own best interests at heart, either.

But that's a thing of the past, starting today.

From here on out, I know where I'm going. I have a mission, and I promise to stick to it, with heart, passion, and compassion. Conflict begone!

I'm not writing this to earn your sympathy. I own my misdeeds and accept that I am paying the price for them. I'm sharing this for the sake of clarity and understanding. I'm sharing so that others might benefit from the lessons I've learned.

After all, we're only human, doing the best we can with the cards we're dealt. Personally, I'd like to see less criticizing, less comparing, less hating on social media. (I've had lots of experience with all of that, believe me, and it needs to stop.)

And I would love to see less judgment of others. Let's focus on the important questions: What do you believe in? What do you cherish? That's what I want to know about you. Those are the meaningful conversations I want to promote, so we can better relate to each other.

I hope you can find it in your heart to forgive me, respect me, and give me another blogging chance.

Because I love you, dear readers, and this time, I promise to not disappoint.

Sincerely yours,

Clementine Liu, a.k.a. Bonjour Girl

I take a no-makeup selfie. The dark circles under my eyes from lack of sleep and the pimples caused by emotional stress are visible. My hair is pulled up in a messy bun, and I'm wearing my most unattractive pyjamas. I sip from Dr. Ho's herbal tea and smile. You can't get more honest, raw, or vulnerable than that. I include the photo in the blog post and hit *publish*.

I'm happy with my post. It was a different approach, and I like it. We'll see what tomorrow brings.

I'm not sure if it's the herbs, the act of writing, or the relief of getting everything off my chest (or a combination of all three), but I fall into the deepest, most restful sleep I've had in ages.

Chapter Thirty-Six

I WAKE UP TO A COLD, half-empty mug of Dr. Ho's herbal concoction sitting on my nightstand. The day after, it smells even funnier, like damp seaweed. For some reason, this makes me smile.

It certainly gave me the boost I needed to write that blog post. I have no idea how all that text poured out of me. Was I somehow channelling some higher source? Or maybe was Cécile giving me the confidence to speak my mind? I managed, after all, to follow the wisdom offered in her book: a lady never retaliates; instead she uses her cunning intellect to find creative solutions to her problems.

I'm not sure what to expect from my readers this morning; I'm anxious, but also strangely calm. Maybe the confidence came from Sandra, who exudes it in spades. She would tell me to go online and face the music like a champion. There's no point just wondering what people think; I need to see the truth for myself.

As soon as I turn on my phone, an insane number of texts, emails, and missed calls flood in. They're from friends, family, Parsons teachers, even total strangers.

Words like "amazing," "OMG," "game changer," and "way to go, Clem!" pop up on my tiny screen. There are messages from Jonathan, Maddie, Jake, and Ellie. Maddie was right. There *is* power in opening up and being vulnerable — much more so than in being defensive. I won't be taking my intuition for granted again.

It's thrilling to see my entire trajectory change with just one blog post.

I open the text from Jonathan first. It's the one I've been waiting for.

My sweet Clementine,

Jake sent me your blog post last night and I just wanted you to know that it made me cry.

You haven't lost me. You could never lose me. On the contrary, you've gained even more of my respect. This blog post shows just how mature you've become and how amazing you are.

I'm sorry that I acted out of insecurity. I didn't feel good about myself, and I was filled with anxiety that I took out on you. You deserve only the best, Clementine.

The "deceptive friend," I assume, is Henry. He sounds like a total A-hole #sorrynotsorry

I'm happy to report that the lawsuit was settled out of court yesterday, and my client pleaded guilty, so I'm off the hook for testifying. But after much reflection, I've told the company to find another photographer — I don't want to be associated with them any longer. I've realized that I need to trust myself. I built this business once, and I can build it back up again. I won't let one bad client define my success.

I can't wait for you to come home so I can hold you in my arms.

I love you, Clementine Liu

J XXOO

I'm shaking and tearing up. I can't believe Jonathan still wants to be with me. I'm not sure I deserve a second chance, but I'm going to take it. He doesn't know yet that I betrayed his trust, but I plan to tell him what happened. I want to be totally honest and transparent with him. That's what lasting relationships are built upon.

I decide to forward his message to Sandra. It's highly personal, but she'll be thrilled to read it, and I trust her completely.

I've got an email from Brian that leaves me speechless:

Dear Clementine,

I read about Bonjour Girl being in the frying pan and I saw your response this morning. It's wise, well-written, and astute. I'm awed by your courage.

I know that I'm the teacher who steered you in the wrong direction. I sincerely apologize. It wasn't my intention to lead you off track. Your blog was out-standing the way it was, and I should have kept my mouth shut. I'm sorry, Clementine.

You taught me a valuable lesson: if something works and is admired by many, why change it?

I've already told Dean Williams and Maddie how much I admire your gutsiness.

With admiration and gratitude,

Brian

Wow. Brian has class. He has my admiration, too. It's Jake's text that takes the cake:

CLEMY, you are one badass blogger, babe! LOVE how you're standing up for yourself while showing your vulnerable side. I love how you don't attack any-one, too. If only more people behaved that way!

I'm learning important things from you, Clem, I really am. No more fighting, and no more hiding. I've gotten on a debt consolidation plan at the bank. I need to move on with my life.

We're shipping the first batch of skirts to your dad tomorrow, so I should be able to make a first payment soon.

Honesty — with yourself and others — really is the best policy. You're my role model, and I think the world of you.

P.S. Sorry Henry turned out to be such a fucking snake. The dude is BUSTED!

LUV you and miss you!

XXOO

This makes me chuckle. I assume that Henry is partly responsible for all this turmoil. I think back to meeting him at the Wild Insect Kingdom and how I unwittingly chose an environment appropriate for his character. Interestingly, I have not yet heard from him. I guess he's doing what snakes do best: slithering away.

Chapter Thirty-Seven

I SHOW UP AT SCHOOL the next day feeling empowered. The overwhelmingly positive response to my blog post has boosted my self-confidence. I haven't lost my credibility after all. I can walk the halls of the Condé Nast Center with my head held high, and that's what matters most. And knowing that Jonathan still cares, despite everything, makes my heart sing. I must be radiating joy from every cell in my body.

I haven't seen or heard from Henry. He's hiding out somewhere, as he should.

Before our digital marketing class begins, Wei beckons for me to follow her out to the hallway.

I wonder what she wants. She's so powerful and commanding, she makes me a bit nervous. I hope I haven't offended her in any way.

"Clementine, I heard what happened to you online, and someone forwarded me your response this morning. I was really impressed with what you wrote."

"Oh, thank you." I try to act cool, but I'm jumping for joy inside. The fact that Wei likes what I wrote confirms that I'm finally on the right path, and that my intuition never lies.

"I was just at the end of my rope," I continue, "and I needed to get that stuff off my chest. I'm tired of being picked on and put down. I just want to spread joy, colour, and creativity in this world, and do it peacefully."

"I have two things to discuss with you, Clementine. First, I want to inform you that your writing assignment has been selected for publication on the website."

"Really? That's fantastic!"

"And second, I want to give your name to the digital ad agency I work with to make you a KOL, a local influencer. I know you are only in China for a short time, but we could make the most of your presence and connect you with local fashion brands for some collaborations. Potentially some really big names."

My mind spins. It's a generous offer, but I know that posting sponsored content just isn't for me, especially after the Victoire & Sophie debacle. After all that's happened, I want to maintain my freedom.

"I'm very flattered, but my goal isn't to become an influencer. I just want to create original content, free from any sponsorship or commercial ties."

Her eyes light up and she puts both hands on my shoulders. "Wow, Clementine Liu. No wonder you have such a loyal following." She smiles broadly, then heads back into the classroom, turning in the doorway to give me one last funny look, as though she has something up her designer sleeve.

I don't know what she's up to, but I trust that her intentions are as pure as shantung silk.

Chapter Thirty-Eight

AFTER CLASS, I SPOT HENRY. He's standing at the far end of the hallway with some friends, looking dishevelled and quite unlike himself. He's wearing an old ratty T-shirt and a checkered shirt over some baggy jeans. I might not have recognized him, except for that unmistakable gaze. He zeroes in on me, and his two friends disappear as soon as they see me coming.

I guess that determined look on my face scared them. Surprisingly, I'm not angry — that feeling disappeared a few days ago, after I pressed the *publish* button on my blog. If anything, I feel sorry for Henry, because if someone needs to stoop that low to get ahead, they must be miserable.

"Can we talk?"

"Sure," he says, staring at the floor.

"Not here."

He follows me to a small, empty classroom. He shuts the door after himself and stoops forward with his hands in the pockets of his jeans.

"I don't know where to start."

"The beginning would be good." I lean against the far wall, keeping my distance. "Wherever the deception started. Because I feel deceived all around."

He pinches the bridge of his nose, clearly holding back tears. I guess I've unmasked him, and it hurts. Whether it's his ego or his heart, I'm not sure.

"God, I feel like such an ass. I'm so sorry, Clementine, I thought Stephen was a good guy. It turns out he wasn't. I had no idea he was up to no good. But since we were partners, I'm as much to blame as he is."

"I'm glad you're owning your shitty mistakes. That's one thing we have in common."

He sits at one of the student desks and takes a deep breath. "Stephen was a venture capitalist in New York. We met at a party there back when I was in college. He wanted to create a portfolio of websites to drum up massive online revenues. He read about these two guys from Hong Kong who were making a killing online and got inspired to do the same. We were planning to build sites for online courses, shopping, a bunch of different platforms. He wanted us to become marketing and digital influencers, too, and hire a whole bunch of people to work for us.

"Then one day, I was surfing the web and came across your blog. I showed it to Stephen — I thought it was so inspiring and original. He started reading your posts and was impressed by the content."

I cross my arms tightly over my chest. This is getting interesting. "I have a feeling I know where this is going." I bite my lip.

"My idea was to ask you to partner with us so we could create a new joint platform for China. That's when I initially reached out to you."

"Yeah, you were laying it on thick as molasses."

He cringes. That's the reaction I was hoping for. He deserves it.

"We were going to make you an offer — a big one — to become an affiliate of ours."

I chuckle to myself. It's nice to feel so in demand. Too bad it's not my cup of jasmine tea.

"But when I heard the forecasts in class that the influencer business was oversaturated, I told Stephen, and we decided to change course."

"Hmm."

"And then, without telling me" — he cringes some more — "he decided to copy your idea and create our own website instead."

"I remember …"

"I told him it was wrong, but his mind was made up. He'd seen the money that could be made and the publicity we could get out of it. Nothing could convince him. I tried to tell myself we could just be friendly competitors, both amplifying similar messages. But when Stephen realized we could never write as engagingly as you, he started playing dirty. He hired people to criticize your content, get it into the hands of *Bloggers Unveiled*, and troll you …"

I purse my lips. I'm trying not to get angry, but it's tough.

"I know you guys are the ones who complained to WeChat about me. Over the blouse you convinced me to accept. Did you purposely connect me with that racist designer, too?" I'm on a roll now.

His face turns the colour of a ladybug. "I was going to pay for the shirt, but the salesperson offered it as a gift. He kept insisting and I finally caved when you were in the change room. I should have said no, or at least told you about it. But I truly didn't think it would matter one way or the other, because you don't typically share stuff like that on your blog. Honestly, I was just trying to impress you. I never thought the store would mention having gifted it to you on their own social media accounts. And I swear, I had no idea that French designer was such a jerk. I'm really sorry about all of it, Clementine. I never intended for things to happen that way." He lets his head fall into his hands. "Things changed for me as I got to know you better. I developed … feelings." He stares down at his shoes.

"Oh, come on, don't bullshit me, okay? I've heard enough of your nonsense already." I roll my eyes. This is getting ridiculous.

"Honestly, I did. I was stuck between you and Stephen."

"You *are* stuck, and you'll stay stuck unless you break free from lousy people who are out to make a quick buck. You're doing things for the wrong reasons."

He lifts his head abruptly. I guess this resonates. Well, if the designer shoe fits …

"Now that I think about it, you aren't really stuck, you just think you are," I continue. "You're as free as a bird but you're keeping yourself chained. It's *your* decision. Whatever you're trying to prove, whoever you're trying to impress, it's not working, okay? You're going down the wrong path. I could make a complaint about you to the school for some of the things you've done, but I'm not going to. I'm taking the high road instead." And without turning around, I walk straight out of his life.

Chapter Thirty-Nine

DESPITE MY FALLING OUT with Henry and the negative association of Jean-Charles's response to our video, I decided to keep the white bag Henry and I customized together. It's a souvenir of a creative moment I'm particularly proud of. I've given the cherry blossom blouse to Ting and Julia at the vintage shop so they can resell it. It may not be old enough to be considered true vintage, but it does have one heck of a backstory.

Those gorgeous embroideries have had me daydreaming about them ever since. Impressed by the skill and craftsmanship that go into creating them, I did a bit of online research and came across an article about a young Chinese woman who left her career as a politician in Shanghai to create this traditional artwork.

Meili Zhou was born to a Miao family in the mountains of Yaoyang, and she successfully made her way to the big city in her twenties. Eventually, though, she quit her high-profile job one day and returned home to learn the embroidery process and start a business dedicated to preserving the art form.

I managed to find Meili online and ask if she would do an interview for *Bonjour Girl*, and she agreed. I was ecstatic. I love telling stories like this. That's all that truly matters to me, not whether the story is obscure enough or should be more mainstream or sponsored.

Now I'm sitting at my desk overlooking the park, interviewing Meili via WeChat video.

"Tell me more about this embroidery. I think more people need to know about it."

"Sure. It's an essential part of Miao culture and a treasure of Chinese costume culture," she says. "Every Miao woman is taught this skill, and it's passed on from generation to generation. Every piece is handmade using a number of complicated skills. It takes at least a year to complete an embroidery one square metre in size, so it's a time-consuming craft that's very hard to make money from."

"Did you learn it from your family?"

"Yes, I learned the skills from my grandmother, my aunts, and my own mother. I started when I was only four, and by the time I was ten years old, I could make a skirt and a shirt by myself."

"Wow. Can you tell me more about the Miao people?"

"The Miao live mainly in the mountains of southern China, in Chongqing and the provinces of Guizhou, Yunnan, Sichuan, Hubei, and Hunan."

"I've read that you had a successful career in politics, but you decided to leave that world."

"Yes, a few years ago, while on a mission for the city of Shanghai, I returned to Chongqing and met some amazing women who reminded me of my cultural identity and reconnected me with these embroidery skills. I visited the Miao villages in Hunan and Guizhou and learned the skills from the masters. I decided to stay for a while and I worked from six in the morning until twelve at night. It was hard work, but well worth it."

"You were basically working much longer hours than you were in politics," I say.

She laughs. "Yes, but loving it. That's the difference. I also researched the current practice of Miao embroidery and collected some of the traditional patterns in order to keep the practice going. That's my mission in life. Two years ago, I finally set up my own company to promote and preserve this folk art. My artwork has been exhibited at home and internationally, too. Now we're partnering with local women's associations to set up training camps."

"And employing women at the same time. That's terrific!"

"You should be applauded, too, for featuring stories that fall outside of traditional fashion."

She promises to send me photos of her work, and with that, we finish our conversation.

A fiercely independent spirit pursuing her passions, Meili is a Bonjour Girl to the core.

Chapter Forty

THIS AFTERNOON, AS soon as I walked through the doors of the Waldorf Astoria Shanghai on the Bund, an exquisite five-star hotel, I knew that this was the setting for that last scene in Henry's video, the one that took away my breath and, unfortunately, a little of my heart.

But it's funny how we've come full circle: his video rendered me speechless, but in the end, I got the last word.

His video did share a powerful message, though: that quote from Lisa See's book about not hiding who you truly are. That sentiment has stayed with me ever since and was instrumental in my breaking free of the expectations of teachers and people on the web.

I'm just happy to be sitting here drinking tea with Sandra, an honest, loyal friend who has my best interests at heart. It feels good to have such a supportive mentor here, since Maddie's not around.

"That was really impressive, what you did, how you so freely expressed yourself on your blog," Sandra says.

"You were instrumental in that, Sandra. You and Dr. Ho. I can't thank you enough. Even his herbs had a positive effect on me, helping me quell my anger and open up."

"I'm so happy to hear it. Dr. Ho is a miracle worker, isn't he? He's been helping me deal with my sister's illness."

"How's she doing?"

"Not good, I'm afraid. The prognosis isn't very encouraging. I just want to be there for her. But it's not easy to see someone you love deteriorate. Heartbreaking, actually. That's why I enjoy spending time with you, Clementine. You bring lightness to my days."

"But I only ever come to you with my own issues — that can't be too refreshing," I say.

"I don't mind. It feels like being back in school, talking about men and clothes — I love it! Speaking of men, what happened to that young man, Henry? Was he the person you referred to in your blog post?"

I look away as I take a sip of tea. I'm still embarrassed to talk about it. "Yes, he was," I mutter. "He turned out to be like those giant teddy bears they sell on the street. Cute and cuddly on the outside, but lacking substance. He was secretly insecure, and he let himself be used. I feel sorry for him now." I heard through some classmates that Henry hasn't set foot in school since we spoke. Not that I wish him any harm, but a little time out reflecting on his actions can only be beneficial to him.

She smiles warmly. "I'm happy to see you're taking this so well."

"I'm learning about trusting people and following my intuition."

"Those are valuable lessons, Clementine."

"I guess. I'm just grateful Jonathan hasn't given up on us."

"That means he really cares about you."

"Yes, he does. Although I'm not sure I deserve him, after what I put him through."

"All relationships go through ups and downs."

"But I feel terrible for flirting with someone else. I did to him the very thing that I accused him of doing last fall. It was unfair, and he didn't deserve it. I can't wait to see him so we can talk face to face."

"You were seduced by the novelty of another person. We all go through that lesson at one point in our lives. Lesson learned."

"Yes, indeed."

"We're all here to learn. That's what life is about. And then we can teach these lessons to others," she says wisely. "And that's what you're doing with your blog."

"Some lessons are more painful than others." I take a sip of tea.

"Yes, they are," Sandra says pensively. "There's something I need to tell you, Clementine. I haven't been completely honest with you."

"Oh?" My mind spins.

"I know how much your mother's infidelities affected you. So if our relationship is to continue to blossom, I have to come clean about what I've been keeping from you …"

I sit up in my chair, taken aback.

"That story I told you on the plane about my great love, Mathias …"

"Yes?"

"His name wasn't really Mathias … It was Christopher. Christopher Liu … your father."

I burst out laughing, but quickly stop, realizing that she's serious. My jaw drops. How can this be?

"Your father was my first and my only significant love. We've remained friends," she says. "It wasn't by chance that we met on the plane. That was orchestrated by your dad," she admits. "He wanted someone to look out for you in Shanghai."

Wow, this feels surreal! An image of my dapper father at a younger age floats through my mind. It's all very strange, but I have to admit that I feel kind of grateful for that.

"As I told you, we met in college and fell madly in love. But we didn't end up together …" she says with regret in her voice. I remember what Sandra said, about me being like the daughter she wished she had. How different would my life have been if Sandra had been my mom? Would my life have been more stable? Maybe not, considering Sandra's finance career. More harmonious? Hard to tell. It sounds like their relationship was a passionate love affair, which doesn't always bode well for stability. As colourful? Probably not …

I decide to drop the what-ifs and just accept things as they are. I'm pleased to know that my dad once loved a woman as amazing and loving as Sandra, and his love life wasn't always so bleak after all.

"We spoke yesterday and agreed that we should tell you," she says.

My mind is still spinning from the news. "This *is* surprising, but pretty cool. I'm happy my father had you in his life."

She just beams as a tear runs down her cheek.

"Thank you."

"Wait, so ... that phone call that came in the car the other day ... was that my dad?"

"No, that was someone else ..."

"Oh, sorry, I didn't mean to pry."

"That's all right." She reaches for a tissue, then changes the subject. "Did you get your WeChat account back yet?"

"Not yet. It can take a really long time, it seems."

"I saw something that might cheer you up." She reaches into her handbag and takes out her tablet to show me a webpage. It's the article I wrote for Wei's class, now published on her fashion website! It's right there, in black and white, next to some stunning photographs of Chinese fashion.

"It's up!"

"This will be great for you and for your profile in China. Lots of people in Shanghai read this website."

"I'm so grateful to Wei for the opportunity to feature my writing." It's a good feeling to have the support of one of the teachers, especially considering the difficulties that surely lie ahead with Jean-Charles.

"And now I have a surprise for you," Sandra says.

"Another one?" What could possibly match finding out about your father's secret love and being published on one of China's leading web platforms?

"This one is bigger!" She signals to someone behind me.

I turn around to look, and it takes me a moment to register who is standing there.

It's Jonathan.

"Oh my god!" I spring to my feet.

"Hello, babe!" Jonathan walks toward me, his arms open wide.

I run to him and let his embrace envelop me completely. It feels so good, like being wrapped in my favourite silk shawl.

He lifts me off the ground and kisses me tenderly. Tears roll down my cheeks.

"Fancy meeting you here!" he says, laughing.

"How did this happen?" I ask, although I've already guessed the answer.

"Jonathan was invited to participate in that photography exhibit I've been working on. He was the one calling me in the car that day …"

This is unreal. Sandra is a philanthropist and a matchmaker. No wonder my father loved her. And I love her, too.

"I also got an unexpected email from one of your teachers, asking me to shoot some pictures for one of her magazines," Jonathan says. "All orchestrated by Sandra, of course."

How amazing. I have not one, but three fairy godmothers: Sandra, Maddie, and Wei.

Jonathan takes a seat at the table. I reach for his hand and hold on tightly. This time, I don't want to let it go. I can't stop grinning. Sandra pours him some tea.

"I told Jonathan I'd fly him to Shanghai on one condition."

"Which was?"

"To take good care of you, Clementine, now that he's settled his affairs. You need some TLC."

"And you're in luck, because that's my specialty," he says, squeezing my hand.

"When did you get here?" I ask Jonathan. "You look so clean and refreshed."

"Sandra booked me a room here last night." I can't believe my ears; her generosity knows no bounds. "But tonight I'm staying with you," he whispers in my ear. He presses his fingers against mine, sending a frisson throughout my body. I smile inwardly. At this moment, I'm wearing that sexy lingerie set I bought before leaving for China. I'd been saving it for the perfect occasion, and strangely enough, I pulled it out of my armoire today.

I guess my intuition is still very much on point.

"I invited Jake, too," Sandra says, "but he said you'd inspired him to settle some things at home."

"Oh, Sandra, that's so kind of you. It's too bad he couldn't make it."

"But we've got him on WeChat video, at least," she says, holding up her tablet.

"Sandyyyy!" Jake's voice screeches from the tablet. "My generous auntie!" He sounds like he's known her for years. "Hello, lovers! I'm so happy you two are reunited." He shimmies on his chair in excitement.

"Yes, it's great to be here," Jonathan says, looking into the screen.

"Sorry I can't be there for the big reunion, but I have business to take care of, thanks to Sandy!"

"Business?"

"I told Sandra about some of my issues and she generously offered to pay for my fabrics and supplies so I can keep doing my thing. *And* she hit up some of her contacts to help me get pre-orders for the capsule collection," Jake says, all smiles. Clearly, he and Sandy have already had a few heart-to-heart conversations. This makes my heart swell.

"You're amazing, Sandra. You really are. And I'm fully committed to the path," Jake says. "Thank you for your big heart and generosity."

"Like I said, I'm thrilled to invest in talented young people like you. And I'm waiting for my skirt," Sandra says.

"It's on its way! Should be there any day now."

"I'll wear it out on the town with Clementine and Jonathan. We have things to celebrate."

I smile back gratefully. Yes, we do. We've only just begun to sample the sublime beauty of this city.

Chapter Forty-One

"I'M SO HAPPY TO BE HERE, Clem. You have no idea how much I missed you. I'm sorry about everything that happened," Jonathan says, holding my hand as we sit side by side on my bed. After our tea with Sandra, Jonathan checked out of the hotel, and we got a taxi back here.

The fact that he apologizes first makes me feel horrible. I should be the one apologizing. It's time to be truthful and tell him what happened with Henry, but I'm worried how he'll react. What if he ends it right here and now? I guess it's a chance I'll have to take.

He senses my hesitation.

"What's the matter, Clementine? Is it something I said?"

"No, of course not. It's … something I *did*."

"Does it … have to do with Henry?"

I nod, not looking up.

"Oh no … did you sleep together?" He jumps off the bed as though it's the scene of a crime.

"No, definitely not!"

"Okay." He sits back down, looking relieved.

"Okay, but we went out to a karaoke bar one night, a group of us, and afterward … he kissed me. And I kissed him back. And I regret it so much." I burst into tears. The guilt has been weighing me down so much. "It meant nothing … I mean, I *was* attracted to him at first, but it was stupid. I should never have risked what you and I have for some fleeting attraction."

Jonathan looks at me, inhaling slowly, measuring his words before he speaks. "Especially to a guy who went on to betray you, huh?"

"Yes," I say, the tears still streaming down my cheeks.

"Listen, Clementine, I want you to know that I forgive you, okay? You kissed some guy while you were out partying. It happens, unfortunately. That's just part of life. But I think you still have some work to do on your trust issues." He caresses my hair softly and wipes away my tears with his thumb. "You need to learn not to sabotage a good thing, to let yourself be loved … by me." He holds my face in his hands. His words stir something deep within me, probably some old childhood wound related to my parents' complicated marriage and the emotional ordeal with my ex-boyfriend in France. Me sabotaging our relationship out of fear of being hurt again … that sounds about right.

"Thank you for forgiving me. It won't happen again. And yes, I will work on things. I don't want to lose you. You mean the world to me."

He kisses me, and then we just sit together, holding each other. Eventually, we lie down and fall into a deep sleep.

In the early hours of the morning, Jonathan discovers my pretty underthings. He runs his fingers down my spine and along the lacy edge of my bra strap, kissing my back tenderly. It feels divine to be held by him, right here in my Shanghai bedroom.

"I love you, Clementine Liu. That twit didn't deserve a kiss from you. From now on, they're all mine, okay?"

My heart nearly explodes. "I love you, too. No more stray kisses, that's a promise!" I kiss him as though we've been apart for decades.

He pulls me in closer and we make love. It's raw and passionate, yet deeply tender. And with each kiss and caress, I feel another layer of the prison I've built around my heart dissolve.

"This is a great idea," Jonathan says. We're sitting and holding hands the Yifu Theatre, the one Michelle Wong suggested visiting. We're here to see a Beijing opera performance of *The Butterfly Lovers* with my Aunt Jiao and my cousins Becky and Emily. I'm wearing the gorgeous skirt Jake made me — this is the perfect venue for it.

According to the program, the theatre was established in 1925. It has featured Beijing opera performances ever since and is favoured by many famous Beijing opera singers. Apparently, in its early days, it was dubbed "the first grand theatre in the Far East." Neither Jonathan nor I know anything about Beijing opera, but he was willing to try something different, and for that I'm grateful.

"Thanks for agreeing to meet my family. My aunt is thrilled," I whisper into his ear. Then I kiss him. I'm on top of the world, especially after our discussion last night. I've realized what a real gem Jonathan is and how immensely lucky I am to have him in my life.

He'll be in Shanghai for ten more days. It'll give us a chance to reconnect and explore some of this magical city together. I've also realized that I still have a lot to learn when it comes to love and to my relationships with others.

On the other side of me, my Aunt Jiao taps my arm. "Here, this is for you." She hands me a note and nods for me to open it. "It's from my husband," she whispers. I nearly fall out of my seat. The last thing I was expecting tonight was a handwritten note from the dragon man.

It's in Mandarin.

> *Dear Clementine,*
> *Congratulations on the publication of your article on one of China's most important websites. Becky showed it to me. That is very impressive — your uncle is proud of you! I want you to know that after reading the article, my son, Vince, told me he no longer wishes to study business. Instead, he wants to study interior design. I told him to be like his cousin Clementine, and just do what makes him happy!*
> *He was the most excited I have ever seen him! Thanks to you, he is happy now. And therefore, so am I.*
> *Uncle Jaw-Long*

I wipe away a tear of joy. If I can be a positive influence on just one single person, it's enough.

"Clementine, I'm sorry for what I said about your mother," my aunt whispers, patting my arm. "That was rude of me. I take it all back."

"That's okay, Aunt Jiao, I know you were just thinking of your brother. My mom really hasn't been the best wife to him. And that girlfriend from college you mentioned?"

"Yes?"

"You were right about her. She is an amazing woman …"

She winks and reaches for my hand. "My brother raised you well. You're turning into a lovely young woman, Clementine," she says.

I smile back gratefully.

I'm willing to experiment and grow, like my teachers want me to, but the most important thing I've learned so far in Shanghai is to be true to myself, no matter what. I can't please everyone, and I don't need to. That's been the best lesson of all.

The curtain finally rises, and I reflect once again on the sublime butterfly, symbol of transformation, growth, and freedom.

Acknowledgements

JUST LIKE CLEMENTINE, who pushed herself beyond her comfort zone to travel and study in Shanghai, in writing this book, so did I. Traveling to faraway places, whether in person or in your imagination, requires a sense of adventure, courage, and a willingness to expand your horizons. Thanks to this series, I am embracing it all.

A big thank you to my manager, Daniaile Jarry, an extraordinary woman who continues to encourage me to reach for the stars. Thank you to Debbie Stasson and Quan Phung for joining along for the magical ride.

Thank you to Scott Fraser, Kathryn Lane, Jenny McWha, Catharine Chen, Elham Ali, and the entire Dundurn team for your dedication, positivity, and amazing spirit. Working with you all is such a treat.

Thanks to my editor Jess Shulman, for the terrific feedback and her continued enthusiasm.

Thank you to Marie-Geneviève Cyr, Nadia Gosselin, Frankie Springer, Sophie Lymburner, Isabelle Rayle-Doiron, Camille Auger, Anna Uvarova, and all those creative souls and friends who inspire me daily.

A massive thank to all my dear friends and family for the support. You are as delicious to me as the delights of Shanghai.